Dancing After Hours

ANDRE DUBUS lives in Haverhill, Massachusetts, and is the author of eight previous books of fiction, as well as *Broken Vessels*, a collection of essays. He received the PEN/Malamud Award, the Jean Stein Award from the American Academy of Arts and Letters, the Boston *Globe*'s first annual Lawrence L. Winship Award, and fellowships from the Guggenheim and MacArthur foundations.

Dancing
After Hours

STORIES BY *Andre Dubus*

PICADOR

I am grateful to the John D. and Catherine T. MacArthur
Foundation; and Frieda Arkin, and Scott Downing;
and the Thursday Nighters, who come to my home
and share their work.

First published 1996 by Alfred A. Knopf, Inc., New York,
and simultaneously in Canada by Random House of Canada Ltd, Toronto

First published in Great Britain 1998 by Picador
an imprint of Macmillan Publishers Ltd
25 Eccleston Place London SW1W 9NF
and Basingstoke

Associated companies throughout the world

ISBN 0 330 35181 8

'Sunday Morning' was originally published in *Boston Review*, 'A Love Song' in *Crazyhorse*,
'All the Time in the World' and 'Dancing in the Dark' in *Epoch*, 'The Timing of Sin' in *Esquire*,
'The Colonel's Wife' in *Playboy*, 'The Intruder' in *Sewanee Review*, 'Falling in Love' in *War, Literature
and the Arts*, 'At Night', 'Blessings', 'The Last Moon', and 'Out of the Snow' in *Yankee*. 'Blessings'
was also published in a limited edition by Raven Editions.

Grateful acknowledgement is made to Warner Bros. Publications U.S. Inc. and Arthur Scwhartz
Music Ltd. for permission to reprint from 'Dancing in the Dark' by Howard Dietz and Arthur Scwhartz,
copyright © 1931 by Warner Bros. Inc. (renewed). Rights for extended renewal term in U.S. controlled
by Warner Bros. Inc. and Arthur Schwartz Music Ltd. All rights reserved. Reprinted by permission of
Arthur Schwartz Music Ltd. and Warner Bros. Publications U.S. Inc., Miami FL 33014.

1 3 5 7 9 8 6 4 2

A CIP catalogue record for this book is available
from the British Library

Printed and bound in Great Britain by
Mackays of Chatham plc, Chatham, Kent

To Jack Herlihy

and in memory of
Richard Yates and James Valhouli

I am grateful to the John D. and Catherine T. MacArthur Foundation; and Frieda Arkin, and Scott Downing; and the Thursday Nighters, who come to my home and share their work.

Martha, Martha, you are anxious about many things.
There is need of only one thing.

—St. Luke 10:41

She thought, Once long ago, I have lived this selfsame
moment, this swoon, and thought how everything is known
at birth, the lather of our begetting, known, then forgotten,
blotted out.

—Edna O'Brien, TIME AND TIDE

Contents

Dancing After Hours

The Intruder

BECAUSE KENNETH GIRARD LOVED HIS
parents and his sister and because he could not
tell them why he went to the woods, his first moments
there were always uncomfortable ones, as if he had left
the house to commit a sin. But he was thirteen and he
could not say that he was going to sit on a hill and wait
for the silence and trees and sky to close in on him, wait
until they all became a part of him and thought and
memory ceased and the voices began. He could only
say that he was going for a walk and, since there was
so much more to say, he felt cowardly and deceitful and
more lonely than before.

He could not say that on the hill he became great,
that he had saved a beautiful girl from a river (the voice

then had been gentle and serious and she had loved him), or that he had ridden into town, his clothes dusty, his black hat pulled low over his sunburned face, and an hour later had ridden away with four fresh notches on the butt of his six-gun, or that with the count three-and-two and the bases loaded, he had driven the ball so far and high that the outfielders did not even move, or that he had waded through surf and sprinted over sand, firing his Tommy gun and shouting to his soldiers behind him.

Now he was capturing a farmhouse. In the late movie the night before, the farmhouse had been very important, though no one ever said why, and sitting there in the summer dusk, he watched the backs of his soldiers as they advanced through the woods below him and crossed the clear, shallow creek and climbed the hill that he faced. Occasionally, he lifted his twenty-two-caliber rifle and fired at a rusty tin can across the creek, the can becoming a Nazi face in a window as he squeezed the trigger and the voices filled him: *You got him, Captain. You got him.* For half an hour he sat and fired at the can, and anyone who might have seen him could never know that he was doing anything else, that he had been wounded in the shoulder and lost half his men but had captured the farmhouse.

Kenneth looked up through the trees, which were darker green now. While he had been watching his battle, the earth, too, had become darker, shadowed, with patches of late sun on the grass and brown fallen pine needles. He stood up, then looked down at the creek, and across it, at the hill on the other side. His soldiers were gone. He was hungry, and he turned and walked back through the woods.

Then he remembered that his mother and father were going to a party in town that night and he would be alone with Connie. He liked being alone, but, even more, he liked being alone with his sister. She was nearly seventeen; her skin was fair, her cheeks colored, and she had long black hair that came down to her shoulders; on the right side of her face, a wave of it reached the corner of her eye. She was the most beautiful girl he knew. She was also the only person with whom, for his entire life, he had been nearly perfectly at ease. He could be silent with her or he could say whatever occurred to him and he never had to think about it first to assure himself that it was not foolish or, worse, uninteresting.

Leaving the woods, he climbed the last gentle slope and entered the house. He leaned his rifle in a corner of his room, which faced the quiet blacktop road, and went to the bathroom and washed his hands. Standing at the lavatory, he looked into the mirror. He suddenly felt as if he had told a lie. He was looking at his face and, as he did several times each day, telling himself, without words, that it was a handsome face. His skin was fair, as Connie's was, and he had color in his cheeks; but his hair, carefully parted and combed, was more brown than black. He believed that Connie thought he was exactly like her, that he was talkative and well liked. But she never saw him with his classmates. He felt that he was deceiving her.

He left the house and went into the outdoor kitchen and sat on a bench at the long, uncovered table and folded his arms on it.

"Did you kill anything?" Connie said.

"Tin cans."

His father turned from the stove with a skillet of white perch in his hand.

"They're good ones," he said.

"Mine are the best," Kenneth said.

"You didn't catch but two."

"They're the best."

His mother put a plate in front of him, then opened a can of beer and sat beside him. He sat quietly, watching his father at the stove. Then he looked at his mother's hand holding the beer can. There were veins and several freckles on the back of it. Farther up her forearm was a small yellow bruise; the flesh at her elbow was wrinkled. He looked at her face. People said that he and Connie looked like her, so he supposed it was true, but he could not see the resemblance.

"Daddy and I are going to the Gossetts' tonight," she said.

"I know."

"I wrote the phone number down," his father said. "It's under the phone."

"Okay."

His father was not tall either, but his shoulders were broad. Kenneth wondered if his would be like that when he grew older. His father was the only one in the family who tanned in the sun.

"And *please*, Connie," his mother said, "will you go to sleep at a reasonable hour? It's hard enough to get you up for Mass when you've had a good night's sleep."

"Why don't we go into town for the evening Mass?"

"No. I don't like it hanging over my head all day."

"All right. When will y'all be home?"

"About two. And that doesn't mean read in bed till then. You need your sleep."

"We'll go to bed early," Connie said.

His father served fried perch and hush puppies onto their plates and they had French bread and catsup and Tabasco sauce and iced tea. After dinner, his father read the newspaper and his mother read a Reader's Digest condensation, then they showered and dressed, and at seven-thirty, they left. He and Connie followed them to the door. Connie kissed them; then he did. His mother and father looked happy, and he felt good about that.

"We'll be back about two," his mother said. "Keep the doors locked."

"Definitely," Connie said. "And we'll bar the windows."

"Well, you never know. Y'all be good. G'night."

"Hold down the fort, son," his father said.

"I will."

Then they were gone, the screen door slamming behind them, and Connie left the sunporch, but he stood at the door, listening to the car starting and watching its headlights as it backed down the trail through the yard, then turned into the road and drove away. Still he did not move. He loved the nights at the camp when they were left alone. At home, there was a disturbing climate about their evenings alone, for distant voices of boys in the neighborhood reminded him that he was not alone entirely by choice. Here, there were no sounds.

He latched the screen and went into the living room. Connie was sitting in the rocking chair near the fireplace, smoking a cigarette. She looked at him, then flicked ashes into an ashtray on her lap.

"Now don't you tell on me."

"I didn't know you did that."

"Please don't tell. Daddy would skin me alive."

"I won't."

He could not watch her. He looked around the room for a book.

"Douglas is coming tonight," she said.

"Oh." He picked up the Reader's Digest book and pretended to look at it. "Y'all going to watch TV?" he said.

"Not if you want to."

"It doesn't matter."

"You watch it. You like Saturday nights."

She looked as if she had been smoking for a long time, all during the summer and possibly the school year, too, for months or even a year without his knowing it. He was hurt. He laid down the book.

"Think I'll go outside for a while," he said.

He went onto the sunporch and out the door and walked down the sloping car trail that led to the road. He stopped at the gate, which was open, and leaned on it. Forgetting Connie, he looked over his shoulder at the camp, thinking that he would never tire of it. They had been there for six weeks, since early June, his father coming on Friday evenings and leaving early Monday mornings, driving sixty miles to their home in southern Louisiana. Kenneth fished during the day, swam with Connie in the creeks, read novels about baseball, and watched the major league games on television. He thought winter at the camp was better, though. They came on weekends and hunted squirrels, and there was a fireplace.

He looked down the road. The closest camp was half a mile away, on the opposite side of the road, and he could see its yellow-lighted windows through the trees. *That's the house. Quiet now. We'll sneak through the woods and get the guard, then charge the house. Come on.* Leaning against the gate, he stared into the trees across the road and saw himself leading his soldiers through the woods. They reached the guard. His back was turned and Kenneth crawled close to him, then stood up and slapped a hand over the guard's mouth and stabbed him in the back. They rushed the house and Kenneth reached the door first and kicked it open. The general looked up from his desk, then tried to get his pistol from his holster. Kenneth shot him with his Tommy gun. *Grab those papers, men. Let's get out of here.* They got the papers and ran outside and Kenneth stopped to throw a hand grenade through the door. He reached the woods before it exploded.

He turned from the gate and walked toward the house, looking around him at the dark pines. He entered the sunporch and latched the screen; then he smelled chocolate, and he went to the kitchen. Connie was stirring a pot of fudge on the stove. She had changed to a fresh pale blue shirt, the tails of it hanging almost to the bottom of her white shorts.

"It'll be a while," she said.

He nodded, watching her hand and the spoon. He thought of Douglas coming and began to feel nervous.

"What time's Douglas coming?"

"Any minute now. Let me know if you hear his car."

"All right."

He went to his room and picked up his rifle; then he saw the magazine on the chest of drawers and he leaned the rifle in the corner again. Suddenly his mouth was dry. He got the magazine and quickly turned the pages until he found her: she was stepping out of the surf on the French Riviera, laughing, as if the man with her had just said something funny. She was blond and very tan and she wore a bikini. The photograph was in color. For several moments he looked at it; then he got the rifle and cleaning kit and sat in the rocking chair in the living room, with the rifle across his lap. He put a patch on the cleaning rod and dipped it in bore cleaner and pushed it down the barrel, the handle of the rod clanging against the muzzle. He worked slowly, pausing often to listen for Douglas's car, because he wanted to be cleaning the rifle when Douglas came. Because Douglas was a tackle on the high school football team in the town, and Kenneth had never been on a football team, and never would be.

The football players made him more uncomfortable than the others. They walked into the living room and firmly shook his father's hand, then his hand, beginning to talk as soon as they entered, and they sat and waited for Connie, their talking never ceasing, their big chests and shoulders leaned forward, their faces slowly turning as they looked at each picture on the wall, at the designs on the rug, at the furniture, passing over Kenneth as if he were another chair, filling the room with a feeling of strength and self-confidence that defeated him, paralyzing his tongue and even his mind, so that he merely sat in thoughtless anxiety, hoping they would not speak to him, hoping especially that they would not ask: *You play football?* Two of them had, and he never forgot it. He had answered with a mute, affirming nod.

He had always been shy and, because of it, he had stayed on the periphery of sports for as long as he could remember. When his teachers forced him to play, he spent an anxious hour trying not to become involved, praying in right field that no balls would come his way, lingering on the outside of the huddle so that no one would look up and see his face and decide to throw him a pass on the next play.

But he found that there was one thing he could do and he did it alone, or with his father: he could shoot and he could hunt. He felt that shooting was the only thing that had ever been easy for him. Schoolwork was, too, but he considered that a curse.

He was not disturbed by the boys who were not athletes, unless, for some reason, they were confident anyway. While they sat and waited for Connie, he was cheerful and teasing, and they seemed to like him. The girls were best. He walked into the living room and they stopped their talking and laughing and all of them greeted him and sometimes they said: "Connie, he's so cute," or "I wish you were three years older," and he said: "Me, too," and tried to be witty and usually was.

He heard a car outside.

"Douglas is here," he called.

Connie came through the living room, one hand arranging the wave of hair near her right eye, and went into the sunporch. Slowly, Kenneth wiped the rifle with an oily rag. He heard Douglas's loud voice and laughter and heavy footsteps on the sunporch; then they came into the living room. Kenneth raised his face.

"Hi," he said.

"How's it going?"

"All right."

Douglas Bakewell was not tall. He had blond hair, cut so short on top that you could see his scalp, and a reddish face, and sunburned arms, covered with bleached hair. A polo shirt fit tightly over his chest and shoulders and biceps.

"Whatcha got there?" Douglas said.

"Twenty-two."

"Let's see."

"Better dry it."

He briskly wiped it with a dry cloth and handed it to Douglas. Quickly, Douglas worked the bolt, aimed at the ceiling, and pulled the trigger.

"Nice trigger," he said.

He held it in front of his waist and looked at it, then gave it to Kenneth.

"Well, girl," he said, turning to Connie, "where's the beer?"

"Sit down and I'll get you one."

She went to the kitchen. Douglas sat on the couch and Kenneth picked up his cleaning kit and, not looking at Douglas, walked into his bedroom. He stayed there until Connie returned from the kitchen; then he went into the living room. They were sitting on the couch. Connie was smoking again. Kenneth kept walking toward the sunporch.

"I'll let you know when the fudge is ready," Connie said.

"All right."

On the sunporch, he turned on the television and sat in front of it. He watched ten minutes of a Western before he was relaxed again, before he settled in his chair, oblivious to the quiet talking in the living room, his mind beginning to wander happily as a gunfighter in dark clothes moved across the screen.

By the time the fudge was ready, he was watching a

detective story, and when Connie called him, he said: "Okay, in a minute," but did not move, and finally she came to the sunporch with a saucer of fudge and set it on a small table beside his chair.

"When that's over, you better go to bed," she said.

"I'm not sleepy."

"You know what Mother said."

"*You're* staying up."

"Course I am. I'm also a little older than you."

"I want to see the late show."

"No!"

"Yes, I am."

"I'll tell Daddy."

"He doesn't care."

"I'll tell him you wouldn't listen to me."

"I'll tell him you smoke."

"Oh, I could *wring* your neck!"

She went to the living room. He tried to concentrate on the Western, but it was ruined. The late show came on and he had seen it several months before and did not want to see it again, but he would not go to bed. He watched absently. Then he had to urinate. He got up and went into the living room, walking quickly, only glancing at them once, but when he did, Connie smiled and, with her voice friendly again, said: "What is it?"

He stopped and looked at her.

"*Red River.*"

He smiled.

"I already saw it," he said.

"You watching it again?"

"Maybe so."

"Okay."

He went to the bathroom and when he came back,

they were gone. He went to the sunporch. Connie and Douglas were standing near the back door. The television was turned off. Kenneth wondered if Connie had seen *Red River*. If she had not, he could tell her what had happened during the part she missed. Douglas was whispering to Connie, his face close to hers. Then he looked at Kenneth.

"'Night," he said.

"G'night," Kenneth said.

He was gone. Kenneth picked up the saucer his fudge had been on and took it to the kitchen and put it in the sink. He heard Douglas's car backing down the trail, and he went to the sunporch, but Connie was not there, so he went to the bathroom door and said: "You seen *Red River*?"

"Yes."

"You taking a bath?"

"Just washing my face. I'm going to bed."

He stood quietly for a moment. Then he went into the living room and got a magazine and sat in the rocking chair, looking at the people in the advertisements. Connie came in, wearing a robe. She leaned over his chair and he looked up and she kissed him.

"Good night," she said.

"G'night."

"You going to bed soon?"

"In a minute."

She got her cigarettes and an ashtray from the coffee table and went to her room and closed the door. After a while, he heard her getting into bed.

He looked at half the magazine, then laid it on the floor. Being awake in a house where everyone else was sleeping made him lonely. He went to the sunporch and latched the screen, then closed the door and locked it. He left the light on but turned out the one in the living room. Then he went to his room and took off everything but his shorts. He was about to turn out the light when he looked at the chest of drawers and saw the magazine. He hesitated. Then he picked it up and found the girl and looked at the exposed tops of her breasts and at her navel and below it. Suddenly he closed the magazine and raised his eyes to the ceiling, then closed them and said three Hail Mary's. Without looking at it, he picked up the magazine and took it to the living room, and went back to his bedroom and lay on his belly on the floor and started doing push-ups. He had no trouble with the first eight; then they became harder, and by the fifteenth he was breathing fast and his whole body was trembling as he pushed himself up from the floor. He did one more, then stood up and turned out the light and got into bed.

His room extended forward of the rest of the house, so that, from his bed, he could look through the window to his left and see the living room and Connie's bedroom. He rolled on his back and pulled the sheet up to his chest. He could hear crickets outside his window.

He flexed his right arm and felt the bicep. It seemed firmer than it had in June, when he started doing push-ups every night. He closed his eyes and began the Lord's Prayer and got as far as *Thy kingdom come* before he heard it.

Now it was not the crickets that he heard. He heard his own breathing and the bedsprings as his body tensed; then he heard it again, somewhere in front of the house: a cracking twig, a rustle of dried leaves, a foot on hard earth. Slowly, he rolled on his left side and looked out the window. He waited to be sure, but he did not have to; then he waited to decide what he would do, and he did not have to wait for that either, because he already knew, and he looked at the far corner of the room where his rifle was, though he could not see it, and he looked out the window again, staring at the windows of the living room and Connie's room, forcing himself to keep his eyes there, as if it would be all right if the prowler did not come into his vision, did not come close to the house; but listening to the slow footsteps, Kenneth knew that he would.

Get up. Get up and get the rifle. If you don't do it now, he might come to this window and look in and then it'll be too late.

For a moment, he did not breathe. Then, slowly, stopping at each sound of the bedsprings, he rolled out of bed and crouched on the floor beneath the window. He did not move. He listened to his breathing, for there was no other sound, not even crickets, and he began to tremble, thinking the prowler might be standing above him, looking through his window at the empty bed. He held his breath. Then he heard the footsteps again, in front of the house, closer now, and he thought: *He's by the pines in front of Connie's room.* He crawled away from the window, thinking of a large, bearded man standing in the pine trees thirty yards from Connie's room, studying the house and deciding which window to use; then he stood up and walked on tiptoes to the chest of drawers and moved his hand over the top of it until he touched the handful of bullets, his fingers quickly closing on them, and he picked up the rifle and took out the magazine and loaded it, then inserted it again and laid the extra bullets on the chest of drawers. Now he had to work the bolt. He pulled it up and back and eased it forward again.

Staying close to the wall, he tiptoed back to the window, stopping at the edge of it, afraid to look out and see a face looking in. He heard nothing. He looked through the windows in the opposite wall, thinking that if the prowler had heard him getting the rifle, he could have run back to the road, back to wherever he had come from, or he could still be hiding in the pines, or he could have circled to the rear of the house to hide again and listen, but there was no way of knowing, and he would have to stand in the room, listening, until his father came home. He thought of going to wake Connie, but he was afraid to move. Then he heard him again, near the pines, coming toward the house. He kneeled and pressed his shoulder against the wall, moving his face slightly, just enough to look out the screen and see the prowler walking toward Connie's window, stopping there and looking over his shoulder at the front yard and the road, then reaching out and touching the screen.

Kenneth rose and moved away from the wall, standing close to his bed now; he aimed through the screen, found the side of the man's head, then fired. A scream filled the house, the yard, his mind, and he thought at first it was the prowler, who was lying on the ground now, but it was a high, shrieking scream; it was Connie, and he ran into the living room, but she was already on the sunporch, unlocking the back door, not screaming now, but crying, pulling open the wooden door and hitting the screen with both hands, then stopping to unlatch it, and he yelled: "Connie!"

She turned, her hair swinging around her cheek.

"Get away from me!"

Then she ran outside, the screen door slamming, the shriek starting again, a long, high wail, ending in front of the house with *"Douglas, Douglas, Douglas!"* Then he knew.

Afterward, it seemed that the events of a year had occurred in an hour, and, to Kenneth, even that hour seemed to have a quality of neither speed nor slowness, but a kind of suspension, as if time were not passing at all. He remembered somehow calling his father and crying into the phone: "I shot Douglas Bakewell," and because of the crying, his father kept saying: "What's that, son? What did you say?" and then he lay facedown on his bed and cried, thinking of Connie outside with Douglas, hearing her sometimes when his own sounds lulled, and sometimes thinking of Connie inside with Douglas, if he had not shot him. He remembered the siren when it was far away and their voices as they brought Connie into the house. The doctor had come first, then his mother and father, then the sheriff; but, remembering, it was as if they had all come at once, for there was always a soothing or questioning face over his bed. He remembered the footsteps and hushed voices as they carried the body past his window, while his mother sat on the bed and stroked his forehead and cheek. He would never forget that.

Now the doctor and sheriff were gone and it seemed terribly late, almost sunrise. His father came into the room, carrying a glass of water, and sat on the bed.

"Take this," he said. "It'll make you sleep."

Kenneth sat up and took the pill from his father's palm and placed it on his tongue, then drank the water. He lay on his back and looked at his father's face. Then he began to cry.

"I thought it was a prowler," he said.

"It was, son. A prowler. We've told you that."

"But Connie went out there and she stayed all that time and she kept saying '*Douglas*' over and over; I heard her—"

"She wasn't out there with *him*. She was just out in the yard. She was in shock. She meant she wanted Douglas to be there with her. To help."

"No, *no*. It was *him*."

"It was a prowler. You did right. There's no telling what he might have done."

Kenneth looked away.

"He was going in her room," he said. "That's why she went to bed early. So I'd go to bed."

"It was a prowler," his father said.

Now Kenneth was sleepy. He closed his eyes and the night ran together in his mind and he remembered the rifle in the corner and thought: *I'll throw it in the creek tomorrow. I never want to see it again.* He would be asleep soon. He saw himself standing on the hill and throwing his rifle into the creek; then the creek became an ocean, and he stood on a high cliff and for a moment he was a mighty angel, throwing all guns and cruelty and sex and tears into the sea.

A Love Song

CALL HER CATHERINE. WHEN HER HEART
truly broke, she was thirty-seven years old, she
had two teenaged girls, and her husband loved another
woman. She smelled the woman's love on his clothes;
it was a perfume she could name but did not. Even the
woman's name, when she learned it from her husband's lips, was not large enough, only two words for
the breath and flesh and voice and blood of only a
woman, only part of what she had traced by smell on
his sweater one night, his jacket another, and traced by
intuition and memory when he was with her and when
he was away at his normal times and when he was away
on the evenings and weekend days he lied about; and
what she had not traced but simply known long before
she smelled another's love on him. Had simply known,

as a person with a disease may know without giving it a name or even notice, long before its actual symptoms and detection.

The woman's name could not encompass what was happening. Nor could the words *love* and *lie* and *sorry* and *you*, nor could her own name on his tongue, on the night he told her in the bright light of their kitchen the color of cream, while upstairs their daughters slept. Nor could tears, nor any act of her body, any motion of it: her pacing legs, her gesturing arms, her hands pressing her face. The earth itself was leaving with her sad and pitying husband, was drawing away from her. Stars fell. That was a song, and music would never again be lovely; it was gone with the shattering stars and coldly dying moon, the trees of such mortal green; gone with light itself.

These words in the kitchen, these smoked cigarettes and swallowed brandy, were two hours of her life. What began as the scent of perfume on wool, then frightened and sorrowful ratiocination that led her beyond his infidelity, into the breadth and depth of the river that was their sixteen years of love—its falls and rushing white water and most of all its long and curving and gentle deep flow that never looked or even felt as dangerous as she now knew it truly was—ended with not even two hours of truth in the kitchen, for truth took most of the two hours to appear in the yellow-white light, and the gray cirrus clouds of blown and rising and drifting smoke, or perhaps took most of the two hours to achieve. Then it was there, unshadowed, in its final illuminance.

Two hours, she figured with pen and paper and numbers, sitting at one in the morning in the kitchen, weeks later, adding and multiplying and dividing, smoking and drinking not brandy but tea: one hundred and twenty minutes that were six ten-thousandths of one percent of her life from the day of her birth until her husband turned his pale and anguished face and walked out the door, into the summer night.

She never again perceived time as she had before, as a child, then an adolescent: a graceful and merry and brown-haired girl, in infinite preparation, infinite waiting, for love; and as a woman loved and in love: with peaceful and absolute hope gestating daughters, and bravely, even for minutes gratefully, enduring the pain of their births; a woman who loved daughters and a man, would bear her daughters' sorrow and pain for them if she could, would give up her life to keep theirs; and loved him with a passion whose deeper and quicker current through the years delighted her, gave at times a light to her eyes, a hue of rose to her cheeks; loved him, too, with the sudden and roiling passion of consolable wrath; and with daily and nightly calm, the faithful certainty that was the river she became until it expelled her to dry on its bank.

For weeks, months, seasons, she was dry, her heart was dry, save with her daughters. Their faces, their voices, their passing touch in a room or hall of the house, their ritual touch and kiss of the days' greetings and good-byes, brought for an instant the earth back to her, and for an instant restored balance to time. Looking into the eyes of a daughter, she actually said to herself, but silently, as though reading the words even as she wrote them in her brain, her heart: *I am here. Now.* Then above the girl's eyes, beyond her head and shoulders, she saw through the window the large green willow, and the darkened grass beneath its hanging branches, and the blue sky. Clearly saw those, and the hazel light of the girl's eyes looking into her own, and listened to the sounds of the girl's voice, giving shape to words about school or a date or a blouse.

This happened often enough with her daughters; then in that first year it began to happen with certain friends: women—one of them, then a second, then a third. Only those three, and not often with them; for most of the time she was with her friends as she was with herself, feeling as though she stood somewhere beside or behind her body, never in front of it. She listened to the sentences she spoke in a low voice that did not rise toward breaking, watched her fingers' patience as they pinched the handle of a cup, spread to hold a cigarette, and did not tremble. In bed at night she lay beneath the weight of herself, held her body up so it would not sink, as it wanted to, into the mattress. She closed her eyes and breathed.

In the eighth month, on a night of gently falling snow, she went to dinner with the three women. The restaurant was expensive and darkened, and her three friends were all happy on the same night, and that was as uncommon as their dressing prettily to go without men to an elegant place. She drank two martinis, then wine, then two cognacs, and everyone was funny and laughing. Then at home she brushed her teeth, watching herself in the mirror, tasting mint foaming with the flavors of garlic and wine and brandy; and she looked at the light in her eyes and the flush of her cheeks, then knew that for the first time in eight months she had had fun. But after that night she was cautious again about drinking, and sipped a glass of wine while cooking and brought it once replenished to dinner, and many nights she drank nothing at all. For she could no longer trust drinking simply to relax her; it could loosen the hold she had on herself; it could break her.

She devoted much of her tenacity to being a good divorced mother. This was the bank of the river. She tried never to malign him before her daughters; sometimes she failed, and apologized. She gave him whatever time with them he wanted; their family life was now one of doors: those of her house, of her husband's car, opening for her daughters' departures and returns. One morning in late winter they went to his wedding.

This was in New England. In April, snow thawed and rain fell and the earth was mud, the sky gray, and the trees and their new growing leaves were dark in the pale light. She wore sweaters and a down vest and boots. Then for two or three days, then for a week, the sky was blue, and the dry sunlit air brightened the leaves and grass. She sat on the patio, drinking a soft drink without sugar, and knew that she longed for spring even as she watched it; she was last April's leaves fallen in autumn, then frosted, then frozen under snow, and in March wet again and becoming part of the earth, while spring was moving before her eyes, leaving her with the other dead it gave life to a year ago, when not only her skin but her heart felt the touch and light of the sun.

For two days in May she turned the soil of a sunlit rectangle of her lawn and planted vegetables and herbs because she wanted to kneel sweating in the dirt and probe it with her fingers and place seeds in it, and she wanted in summer to watch the green plants grow, white and pink radishes push upward into light, tomatoes green, then yellow, then red on the vines.

Her first lover surprised her: his existence did, his passion; hers. They met by chance in a video store. When she told her friends, they were happy; plans shone in their eyes, hopes. She had none. All three were divorced; all three wanted husbands, or at least—or perhaps better still—a constant and honorable lover. That was in their eyes, the corners of their mouths. They came to believe that she looked upon love for a man as an ephemeral passion. They marveled; they envied; and she watched herself and her friends, and listened to their words and hers, and wondered why none of them saw in her eyes and at the corners of her lips the dark glisten and static quiver of stored tears.

The man was pleasant and humorous enough; he was flesh. Her friends were right about this: she delighted in making love only for the act itself, the sensations that did not touch her heart. At times, dressing at the mirror, waiting for him, she felt like the woman her friends thought her to be. He was divorced, a father of two small children, and when he declared his love and spoke of marriage, she stopped seeing him.

At a Christmas party, she met a man who became her lover for years. His first wife had hurt him deeply, with lies and infidelity, then the prolonged assault of divorce for the rest of his life, denying him his children but for the scant time allowed by the court, and telling his children that he was the adulterer, the liar, and taking the house and half of everything else; he would never again marry. He would never again live with a woman. She learned all of this while drinking two

Manhattans at the party; then she went home with him, to his apartment without plants or flowers or feminine scents, a place that seemed without light, though its windows were tall and broad; then she knew why: it was not a place where someone lived; he ate and slept there and did this in his double bed, did this tenderly, wickedly; his home was like an ill-kept motel.

They did not become a couple. They were rarely together more than twice a week, and never slept together, to wake to the harsh or tender or surprising light of morning. Her daughters married, and at the receptions she was polite with the woman whose perfume she had smelled years ago as she embraced her husband. The weddings were three years apart, and at both of them she watched the girl in white, and with belief and hope she raised a hand to her slow tears, pressed and brushed them with her fingers as joy spread through her, filling her, so her body felt too small for it, and she deepened her breath to contain it, to compress it, to keep it in place in her heart.

Falling in Love

T ED BRIGGS CAME BACK FROM THE WAR
seven years before it ended, and in spring two
years after it ended he met Susan Dorsey at a cast party
after a play's final performance, on a Sunday night, in
a small town north of Boston. He did not want to go to
the play or to the party, but he was drinking with Nick.
They started late Sunday afternoon at the bar of a Boston steak house. In the bar's long mirror they watched
women. Nick said: "Come with me. My sister likes it."

"She's directing it."

"She's hard to please."

"What's the play?"

"I forget. Some Frenchman. You'd know the name."
Ted looked at him. "It sounds like another word.

Which isn't the point. The party is the point. These theater people didn't need the sexual revolution."

"I don't have to see a play to get laid."

"Why are you pissed off? You act benighted. You're always reading something; you go to plays." Nick motioned to the bartender, then waved his hand at the hostess standing near the front door; when she looked at him, he signaled with his first two fingers in a V and pointed to the tables behind them. Ted looked at his fingers and said: "It's that."

Nick lowered his hand to the bar and said: "It's what?"

"The peace sign. I was at a party once, with artists. People asked about my leg. I told them. They were polite."

"Polite."

"It was an effort."

"For them."

"Yes."

"Hey, we're lawyers. They'll hate both of us."

Ted looked at Nick's dark and eager face and said: "We can't let our work keep us home, can we?"

"Men like us."

"Men like us."

Ted Briggs was a tall man with a big chest and strong arms and a thick brown mustache, and Susan Dorsey liked his face when she saw him walk into the party, into the large and crowded living room in an apartment she had walked to from the theater where she had worked so well that now, drinking gin and tonic, she felt larger than the room. She did not show this to anyone. She acted small, modest. She was twenty-two and had been acting with passion for seven years, and she knew that she could show her elation only to someone with whom she was intimate. To anyone else it would look like bravado. Her work was a frightening risk, and during the run of the play she had become Lucile as fully as she could, and she knew that what she felt now was less pride than gratitude. She also knew this fullness would leave her, perhaps in three days, and then for a while she would feel arid and lost. But now she drank and moved among people to the man with a drink in his left hand, his right hand resting on a cane, his biceps filling the short sleeves of his green shirt. Beside him was a shorter and older man with dark skin and black curls over his brow. She stopped in front of them and said her name, and knew from their eyes that they had not seen her in the play. Nick's last name was Kakonis. Ted leaned his cane against his leg and shook her hand. She looked at his eyes and said: "Did you like the play?"

"We just got here," Nick said, and Ted said: "What was it?"

"*The Rehearsal.* By Jean Anouilh."

"*That* Frenchman," Nick said.

"I like his plays," Ted said. "Were you in it?"

"I was Lucile."

"We got lost," Ted said.

They got lost in vodka, in wine with their steaks, in cognac; then Nick drove them out of the city and north. Once they had to piss and Nick left the highway and stopped on a country road, and they stood beside the car, pissing on grass. Then he drove on the highway again; they talked about work and women, and time was not important. They were leaving the city and going to the cast party. If the play started on time, the curtain had opened while they were driving out of Boston. When they reached the town and found the theater, they were an hour and five minutes late; they drank coffee at a café and, through its window, watched the theater's entrance across the brick street. When people came out, Ted and Nick went to the theater, and in the lobby, among moving people, Nick found his sister, a large woman in a black dress; her face was wide and beautiful, and she said to Nick: "Asshole."

Then she hugged him and shook Ted's hand. Her name was Cindy. They walked on brick sidewalks to the apartment of the stage manager, who taught drama at a college. The air was cool and Ted could smell the ocean; he felt sober and knew he was not. Outside the apartment, an old two-story house, he heard voices and a saxophone solo. They climbed to the second floor and Cindy introduced them to people standing near the door, and left them. Ted and Nick went to the long table holding liquor and an ice chest and poured scotch into plastic glasses. They stood with their backs to a window and Ted looked at a young red-haired woman in a beige dress walking toward him, looking at his eyes, and smiling. He exhaled and for a moment did not breathe.

Then she was there, looking at him still; her eyes were green; she looked at Nick and said: "Susan Dorsey," and gave him her hand. Ted leaned his cane against his leg and took her hand. For the rest of the party he stayed with her, except to go to the bathroom; to go to the table and pour their drinks, stirring hers with the knife he used to cut the lime; to go to Nick and say "Excuse me" to the woman Nick was with; to turn Nick away from her and say in his ear: "Does this town have a train station?"

Nick put his arm around Ted and squeezed.

"You don't need one," he said. "She lives in Boston."

"How do you know?"

"Cindy told me. I might be heading a bit farther north. How do I look?"

"You look great."

At one o'clock Susan finished her gin and tonic, and when Ted took her glass, she said: "I'll have a Coke."

She was afraid of dying young. She had talent and everything was ahead of her and she was afraid it would be taken away. This fear came to her in images of death in a car, in a plane. There was no music now, and people had been speaking quietly since eleven, when the stage manager asked them to remember his neighbors. She watched Ted walking toward her, her glass and his in the palm of his left hand. A shell from a mortar had exploded and flung him off the earth and he had fallen back to it, alive. She wanted to be naked, holding him naked. She took the Coke from his hand and said: "I need an hour. I don't want to drive drunk."

"Are you?"

"It's hard to tell, after working."

Her car was small, and when they got in, he pushed his seat back to make room for his leg; its knee did not bend. She pushed her seat back and turned to him and held him and kissed him. She liked the strength in his arms hugging her. She started the car and left the seat where it was; only the upper half of her foot was on the gas pedal. She drove out of the town and through wooded country and toward the highway, then said: "You have very sad eyes."

"Not now."

"Even when they twinkle. You wanted to be a corpsman."

"It wasn't what you think. I joined the Navy to get it over with, on a ship. Before I got through boot camp, I felt like a cop-out. Then I asked to be a corpsman and to go with the Marines. A lot of times at Khe Sanh, I wished I had just joined the Marines."

"So you could shoot back?"

"Something like that. Were you good in the play?"

Yes filled her, and she closed her lips against it and reached into her purse on the floor, her arm pressing his leg; then she put her hand on the wheel again and looked at the tree-shadowed road and said: "I forgot to buy cigarettes."

"From a squirrel?"

He lit one of his Lucky Strikes and gave it to her and she drew on it and inhaled and held it, but the smoke did not touch what filled her. She blew it out the window and said: "I was great in the play."

After he came home from the war, making love was easy. He had joined the Navy after his freshman year at Boston College, because his mind could no longer contain the arguments and discussions he had had with friends, most of them boys, and with himself since he was sixteen years old. One morning he woke with a hangover and an instinct he followed to the Navy recruiting office. When he came home from the war and eight months in the Navy hospital in Philadelphia, kept there by infections, he returned to Boston College and lived in the dormitory. He had made love in high school and college before the war, but the first time with each girl had surprised him. After the war he was not surprised anymore. He knew that if a girl would come to his room or invite him to hers or go on a date with him, off the campus, walking in Boston, she would make love. There were some girls who did not want to know him because he had been in the war and his cane was like a uniform. Few of them said anything, but he saw it in their eyes. He felt pain and fury but kept silent.

There were boys like that, too, and men who were his teachers, people he wanted to hit. In his room he punched a medium bag and worked with weights. Sometimes, drunk in bed with a girl, he talked about this until he wept. No girl could comfort him, because the source of his tears was not himself. It was for the men he knew in the war, the ones he bandaged, the ones he saved, the ones he could not save; and for the men who were there for thirteen months and were not touched by bullets, mortars, artillery. "They're not abstractions in somebody else's mind," he said one night to a girl; and, holding her, he said aloud some of their names; for him they were clearly in the dark room; but not for her. Then looking at her face, he saw himself in the war, bandaging and bandaging and bandaging, and he stopped crying. He said: "How the fuck would you like to be hated because you did a good job, without getting killed?" This one soothed him; she said she'd want to kill somebody.

Now he was twenty-eight and it was still easy; it

could be counted on; he only had to invite a woman to go someplace, for a drink, or dinner. The women decided quickly and usually he could see it in their eyes within the first hour of the date. If they felt desire and affection, they made love. Susan would, too. They were on the highway now and he looked at her profile. He was drunk and in love. Nearly always he felt he was in love on his first night with a woman. It happened quickly, as they drank and talked and glanced at menus. It lasted for months, weeks, sometimes days. He touched Susan's cheek and said: "Maybe I should court you. Bring you flowers. Hold your hand in movies. Take you to restaurants, and on picnics. Kiss you good night at your door."

"You've got about twenty minutes. Maybe twenty-five."

Lying beside him, using the ashtray he held on his chest, she wanted to feel what she was feeling, had wanted to for a long time, this rush of love, pulling her up the three flights of stairs to her small apartment, into the bathroom for the diaphragm she had used often this year with different men, but now her heart was full, as it had not been for over a year, and she was not certain whether it was love that filled her or so wonderfully being Lucile and ending that work with this strong man with sad eyes and a bad knee and a history she could feel in his kiss. When they made love, she could feel the war in him, could feel him ascending from what he had seen, what he had done; from being blown up. Her heart knew she was in love. She said: "I like you a lot."

"But what?"

"Nothing. Am I going to see you again?"

"Has that happened to you?"

"Of course it has. I'm easy. So are you."

"You'll see me a lot. Let's have dinner tonight. French—for the play."

"That you missed."

"We weren't lost. We drank too much. We talked too much."

"And you both got lucky."

"I think I got more than lucky."

"You did. I wish you had seen me."

"So do I. I'll see the next one, every night."

"It's at the Charles Playhouse. We start rehearsals in two weeks." He moved the ashtray to the bedside table and she put her hand on his chest and looked at his eyes. "After that I'm going to New York. Last month I got an agent."

"Good. It's where you should be."

"Yes. I want all of it: movies too."

"New York is just a shuttle away."

"I hope more than one."

She kissed him; she held him.

He ate lunch with Nick. They wore suits and ties. He had slept for two hours, waked at seven to Susan's clock radio, turned it off before she woke, phoned for a cab he waited for on the sidewalk, gone to his apartment to shower and shave and dress, and then walked to his office. At nine o'clock he was at his desk. Nick came forty minutes later, and stopped at Ted's door to smile, shrug, say: "Lunch?"

At lunch Nick ordered a Bloody Mary, and said: "I hate Monday hangovers. You don't have one."

Ted was drinking iced tea.

"No. I was drunk when we left the party. But I didn't drink again and I was awake till five. By then I was sober."

"We drank."

"I don't drink for a hangover anyway. I cure it with a workout. Susan's going to New York."

"Permanently?"

"Nothing's permanent. She's an actress."

"New York's not far."

"Hollywood is."

"How do you know she's that good?"

"A hunch."

"What happened?"

"I spent the night with her."

"But what happened? Two weeks ago you said you wanted a girlfriend you saw on weekends. You may even have said *some* weekends. Even if she gets Hollywood, they take her out of thousands of pretty young actresses, that sounds like a weekend to me."

"I want her to get Hollywood; I want her to get Broadway. And I want her."

He was with her every night and, before her rehearsals started, they met for lunch and drank martinis and he was out of his office for two hours. On weekends he made picnic lunches and drove with her to the ocean. The water was cold, but the sun was warm and they wore sweatshirts and sat on the beach. At night they ate in restaurants and they made love and slept in her apartment or his. When she started rehearsals, she did not have time for lunch, and all day as he worked, he waited to see her. "I'm easy," she had said, and when he imagined her living in New York, working as a waitress, rehearsing with men, he could not bear it. He knew she loved him and he believed she wanted to be faithful to him; but she was beautiful and a hedonist and there would be men trying to make love with her, and she would feel something for some of them. Without telling her, he tried to give her license, tried to imagine a situation he could accept: if she were drunk one night in New York and it happened only that night.

But it would not be one night with one man. By now he had seen her in the new play. She played the youngest sister, Beth, in a large family gathered at the mother's home while the mother died. Beth was the one who had not moved away; had stayed in the small town and lived near her mother, and cared for her when she was sick, as she had cared for her father. The others lived far away and were very busy and usually drunk. Beth was twenty-nine and Ted believed the playwright had given her age and her not having a lover more importance than they deserved, as though she were Laura in *The Glass Menagerie;* but Susan made Beth erotic and lonely and brave, and you knew she would have a lover, in time, when she was ready, when she chose to; and Ted knew that, unless Susan was very unlucky, she would work in New York and in Hollywood. So it would not be one night drunk with one man; Susan was going on the road for the rest of her life.

She had a toothbrush now in his apartment, a robe, a nightgown, a novel she was reading. Two weeks before the play closed, she had a yard sale, let go of her apartment, and moved into his. It was large and from its living room he could see the Charles River. When the play closed, his pain began; but he was excited, too, about weeknights and weekends in New York, and about Susan acting there. And he believed she had greatness in her, and he wanted to see it. On a Friday afternoon near sunset, they stood at his windows, looking at the river and Cambridge. She said: "I have to do something before I go to New York. I'm six weeks pregnant."

He looked at her eyes, and knew that what was falling inside him would not stop falling till it broke. He said: "No."

"No what? I'm not pregnant? Did you think you were shooting blanks?"

"No, don't do it."

"I'm twenty-two years old, I'm going to New York, and you want me to have a fucking baby?"

The falling thing in him hit and broke and he trembled and said: "Not a fucking baby. Our baby, Susan. Our baby."

He had to look away from the death of everything he saw in her eyes.

She looked at the river. Since seeing her doctor in the middle of the afternoon, she had felt very unlucky and as sad as she had ever been; now Ted was begging her to marry him. No one had ever asked her to marry, or even mentioned it, and Ted was begging for it. Finally she looked at him. She said: "It has nothing to do with marriage. I can't even think about marriage. I don't want a baby. Why can't you understand that?"

"Then have it, and give it to me."

"Have it? *You* have it."

"Seven and a half months. That's all I'm asking."

"You think it's numbers? A fucking calendar? You want me to go through all of that so you can have a baby? Go find somebody else to breed with."

"I did. Now you want to kill it."

"I don't *want* to kill anything. What I want is not to be pregnant. What I want is never to have fucked you."

"Well you did. Now it's time for some sacrifice. Okay? Maybe pain, too. And what's new about *those.* For just seven and a half months. Of your life you think is so fucking significant."

She raised her hand to slap his face, his glare, his voice, but she did not; all the bad luck and sadness she had felt till she told him filled her, and his face enclosed her with it, and she felt alone in a way she had never felt alone before. She did not want to be alive. Then she was crying and with her raised hand she covered her eyes. He touched her arms and she recoiled, stepped back, wiped her tears, and opened her eyes.

"You don't know anything," she said. "You think I could have a baby and not love it? Are you that stupid? I can't love a baby. Not now. I thought I could love you. That was enough."

"You don't love anyone."

"Yes I do. And I didn't mean I wished I had never fucked you. But I won't fuck you again. War hero with your cane. *Sac*rifice. *Pain.* Don't *ev*er think I don't know about those. Don't *ev*er think you're the only one in pain. Do something for me. Leave. I'm going to Cindy's. I don't want you here while I pack. Lurking around and crying and asking me to change my life. Okay? Just leave. Go drink someplace. You're good at that."

She wanted something different. She could not imagine what it was: some transformation, of Ted, of herself, of time. He said: "You're good at evicting."

He walked out, and she phoned Cindy and said: "Cindy?" then sobbed.

Soon she was in New York, but for a long time a desert was inside her; it was huge and dry and there was nothing in it. Someday she would get an intrauterine device, but not now; maybe later in the summer, or in the fall. First she needed work to flood that dry sand.

On a summer evening Ted went to dinner with Nick, then to Fenway Park to watch the Red Sox play the Orioles; it was a very good game, well pitched and intense, and till the Red Sox lost in the ninth, with the tying run on third and the winning run on second, Ted's sorrow was not deep; was only a familiar distraction like his knee, which kept his leg in the aisle. He had drunk martinis with Nick before dinner and wine with dinner and they drank beer during the game. Then Nick walked with Ted to his apartment and they rode the elevator upstairs. Ted poured two snifters of cognac and held their stems in his left hand and took them to the living room, where Nick stood, looking out the open windows. Ted said: "That's where she was, the last time I saw her. We were looking at the river."

He felt alert, but his left knee bent now and then, on its own, and he knew he was drunk. When he drank a lot, he drank standing: his right knee was useless as a signal, but the left one warned him. The sounds of car engines rose from the street, and faint voices of people walking. Nick said: "What's it been? A month?"

"Five weeks tonight."

Ted raised the snifter and breathed the sharpness of the cognac, tasting it before he drank; then he drank. He looked over the glass rim at Nick, drank again and looked at light reflected on the dark river, looked across it at the lights of Cambridge. He said: "Then she went to the abattoir. 'The old men are all dead. It is the young men who say yes or no. . . . The little children are freezing to death. . . .'" He knew Nick was watching him, but he could not feel Nick watching; he felt the lucidity and eloquence of grief let out of its cage by drinking. "'I want to have time to look for my children and see how many I can find. Maybe I shall find them among the dead. . . . I am tired; my heart is sick and sad. From where the sun now stands I will fight no more forever.'"

Closing his eyes, he saw Susan's face, felt that if he opened them quickly, but at the right moment out of all the night's moments, her face would be in front of him; she would be standing here. Nick said: "That was good. Chief Joseph."

Ted opened his eyes and said: "I used to know the whole thing." He looked away from the river, at Nick, and said loudly: "You know what I say, Nick? From where the sun now stands I will ejaculate no more forever in the body of a woman who will kill our child," and saying it, and saying it loudly, released all the grief, as something he felt he could see, touch, in the air before his face, and now he felt only rage, and the strength and conviction it brings; it filled him, and his arms and cognac and cane rose with it, his mouth opened to cry out with it; he saw Nick and the windows, but he did not see them; then it was gone, as the flame of a candle is blown out, and the gentle breath that dispelled it was a woman's. She was many women; she was any woman whose eyes, whose touch, whose voice, whose lips would draw him again, and he closed his mouth and lowered his arms, lowered his head. He looked at Nick's brown loafers, feeling only helpless now; and ashamed, knowing what a woman could do to him, knowing she could do it because he wanted her to. Then Nick's hand was on the back of his neck, squeezing, and Nick said: "You've got to start dating again. This time get one on the pill."

Ted looked at him, tossed his cane onto the couch, and held Nick's arm. He said: "The pill isn't a philosophy. I need a philosophy to go out there with. You know? I can't just go out there with a cock, and a heart. Maybe I need a wife."

"Wives are good. I'd like a wife. I'm two baseball seasons from forty. Do you know at the turn of the century, in America, the average man lived forty-seven years? For women, it was forty-six. Maybe a wife is what you need."

"I need a vacation."

"You've been on one for five weeks."

"Not from women. From women, too. I mean two weeks someplace. Mexico. Alone. I don't speak Spanish. I can order from a menu. But I won't understand the rest. I'll be alone. I need to think, Nick. All I've been doing is feeling. Find a village near an airport. Something in the mountains. Bring some books, have one drink before dinner, maybe a beer while I eat. Hole up, walk around; be silent. Look the demon in the eye."

Nick rubbed his neck and said: "Drink bottled water. Peel the fruit. Don't shit your brains out."

"If I did, all you'd see in the bowl is water."

"Stop that. It's just something that happened. And leave the demon here. You've looked at it enough."

"No. I haven't looked at it. I've fucked it. Now I'm going to look at it; talk to it."

Holding Nick's arm, he closed his eyes and pressed the back of his neck into Nick's hand.

Blessings

FOR MADELEINE

ARLY IN THE MORNING ON THE FIRST
anniversary of the day her family survived, the
mother woke. At first she thought it was the birds. In
the trees near the cabin, their songs in the early twilight
were too sharp, more a sound of intrusion or alarm
than the peace she and Cal had rented for two weeks
on this New Hampshire lake. She had never liked to
wake early, and on most days of her adult life she woke
before she was ready, and needed coffee and a cigarette
at once. But in this early morning, in the gray beginning of light, she was awake and alert as though in evening, when her body was most vibrant, when she and
Cal drank their two martinis, sometimes three, and she
told him of the birds and animals she had seen that
day (pheasants lived on their Massachusetts land; foxes

stalked them; and there were birds in the trees and at her feeder and pecking on the earth below it), and whom she had seen and what she had heard, and the questions and answers or attempts at them she had stored up in her silent monologues with herself. Much of the time these were dialogues with Cal, though she was alone in the house or on their land or cross-country skiing on the meadow across the road or walking long and fast in trails through woods. Cal would often interrupt her, smiling, watching her, and ask: "What did I say to that?" To her wondering whether families and America were worse now than when she and Cal were children, or even when their own daughter and son were children, or if all this horror of children beaten and raped at home, or kidnapped for pornographic pictures and movies, or for the erotic and murderous desires of one man, was nothing new at all, and only the reporting of it in newspapers and magazines and television was new. Or why those women, certainly with good intentions, were trying to stop a supervised hunt ordered by the game-management people to kill some of the weak among too many deer in a small state-protected woods in a neighboring town, the women threatening—and not bluffing, she knew, and with good intentions, she knew—to go in with the hunters and stand in front of their shotguns to save the deer, and even insisting that if the deer starved to death that winter, it was not only nature's way but painless. Why didn't they know that, having killed or run off for buildings and asphalt the deer's natural predators, people had to perform the function of coyotes and wolves? She also, on those evenings, entertained Cal, made him laugh at her anecdotes about the supermarket, or traffic, or phone calls from friends. By evening, Cal's body and mind were near the state of hers when the alarm clock woke her, and, as relaxed and cheerful as he might be, he looked in need of a nap until midway or more through his first martini. Her name was Rusty. It had been Margaret until Cal Williams met and courted her when she was twenty-one and he was twenty-three; he had called her Rusty, because of her hair, because he was in love with her, and it had become her name.

He was sleeping on his right side now, his face toward her, his left hand resting on her stomach. Below his hand her legs were tensed to spring from the bed, to run not from but at an intruder in the room, while her hand grabbed whatever weapon it could to swing at his face; beneath Cal's hand her stomach rose and dropped with her accelerated breath, and she felt her heart beating with that adrenaline they now said could kill you, if you were sedentary, if your heart were accustomed to a soft cushion of quotidian calm. Hers was not; but even if it were, she knew the thought of a heart attack would still be as distant as their home among the pines and poplars and maples and copper beeches on the long, wide hill. For she knew it was not the birds that had alerted the muscles in her legs and arms and the one beating beneath her ribs, ready to fight the intruder her body was gathered for, the intruder she had known when she first woke was not there; it was the day itself that woke her: the fourteenth of July.

It had waked her before, while Cal slept as he did now, as he had on that night one year ago when the day ended and she and Cal and Gina and Ryan had showered the salt water and perhaps some of the terror from their bodies, had eaten even, for they were very hungry, and their bodies were frail, too, with a weakness that food alone could not strengthen, and in the restaurant in Christiansted they had drunk a lot, all of them, before and during and after dinner. Then Gina had gone to her room in the hotel and Ryan to his, and she and Cal had gone to bed, and soon Cal was asleep, while she smoked and listened to Gina and Ryan settling in their rooms on either side of hers, and she knew Cal slept so easily not because he was oblivious but because his body was more in harmony with itself and life, and death, than hers. His family had survived. The young captain and mate were dead, the captain at least ashore now to lie beneath a monument marking his passage on earth and his possession of his final six feet of it, while the mate was forever in the Caribbean, swallowed by its creatures, parts of him—some bones, perhaps even flesh (where was his head, his face?)—left to sink, to become parts of the bottom of the sea, parts of the sea itself. Cal's body and mind and heart had endured that, and in bed after dinner they demanded of him, as they should, as hers could not or would not, that he sleep. For a week after his mother's death, when he was forty-eight, he skipped the evening drinks, ate early and with the effort of a tired child, and was in bed sleeping by seven.

For a long time that night a year ago, she did not sleep. Once she heard Gina flush the toilet and she looked at her traveling clock on the bedside table and it glowed two-fifteen at her; at three-twenty Ryan flushed his toilet. And both times she heard the children drop heavily into their beds and the sleep their bladders had barely disturbed; and each time she qui-

etly and briefly wept, for their sounds recalled to her
the nights of Gina's and Ryan's growing up when she
woke hearing them walking down the hall to their
rooms, their light footsteps only audible when the
flushing that woke her had ceased and she could hear
the moving weight of their small warm bodies above
the faint sound of water filling the tank. Her weeping
that night in the hotel at St. Croix was soundless, her
tears so few they did not even leave her eyes which she
wiped dry with the sheet, and it was neither joyful nor
frightened nor relieved: it simply came, as milk had
once come from her breasts.

Sometime after three-twenty she slept. They stayed
one more week on the island, to answer questions and
sign statements, to attend the captain's funeral, a young
blond man from California whose young blond, tanned
woman wore a white dress and sat with his family in
the front pew—a father and mother and two older
brothers, who arrived in three different planes from the
United States and wore black—and all through the
service she stared at the casket, her face still lax with
the disbelief that for others becomes in moments a
truth they must bear all their lives. Then at the grave,
as the brothers at her sides turned her tall, strong body
away from the open hole where the captain lay under
flowers, the young woman having plucked the first
from a wreath and dropped it onto the casket, she col-
lapsed: her knees bent, her body fell, and the two
brothers strained to hold her as, doubled over, her lowered face covered by the long blond hair fallen forward
and down, she keened.

Rusty and Cal and Gina and Ryan attended the
memorial service for the mate, who was from Rhode

Island, whose family arrived on five planes: two sisters, a brother, the mother and her husband, the father and his wife. Rusty sensed that the mate had not had a lover on the day of his death, but there were two young women, one in blue, one in gray, in the pew behind the family, and something about the way they entered together, and sat close, and glanced from time to time at each other, and lowered their faces to cry, either simultaneously or the tears of one starting the tears of the other, made Rusty believe they had at one time, separately but probably in quick succession, been the mate's lovers; and whether the one in blue had taken the place of the one in gray in the mate's heart, or the other way around, they were joined for at least this bodiless service, perhaps even because it was bodiless, and for these minutes in the church were somehow united as sisters are, even sisters who dislike each other but despite that are bound anyway because they will never again see or hear or touch someone they both loved. The memorial service was the day after the captain's funeral, and the questions and answers and signing of statements for the Coast Guard lieutenant from Puerto Rico were done, but the family stayed for the remainder of the week, because they had planned to.

They had planned those fourteen days while eating dinner in Massachusetts, when the thermometer outside Rusty's kitchen window was at twelve degrees and there was a wind from the north and Cal had said: "If we wait till the off-season I can pay for the whole thing. For everybody." Gina and Ryan, both working, renting apartments, buying cars, had happily, gratefully, protested; and agreed when Cal said: "Or we can all go Dutch this week." During those final days at St. Croix they swam in the small pool at the hotel, but none of them went into the sea, whose breakers struck a reef a short distance from the beach, a natural shield against both depth and sharks, so that only a tepid, shallow pool with the motion of a lake reached the sand at the hotel. One evening, from the outdoor bar, Rusty watched Gina standing with a tall sunset-colored rum drink on the beach, near the water; she stepped toward it once, and stopped paces from where it touched the sand. Then she stepped back and smoked a cigarette and finished her drink, looking beyond the reef at the blue water and the half-disk of red sun at its horizon. Rusty watched the sun until it was gone, and green balls rose from the spot where it sank; they seemed shot into the sky like fireworks, and she thought of the mate scattered in the sea.

That fourteenth of July had waked Rusty on nights in the final months of last year's New England summer, and in the autumn, when she could smell the changes in the cooler air coming through the windows: a near absence of living plants and trees, the air beginning to have the aroma of itself alone, as it did in winter, when still she woke, not every night or even every week, and lay in the room with the windows closed and frosted, her face pleasantly cold, and listened to the basement furnace, its thermostat lowered for the night, pushing heated air through the grates in the house. In that first spring she woke in the dark and breathed air tinged with the growth of buds and leaves and grass beyond her windows. Now it was the anniversary of the day itself, and she and Cal and Gina and Ryan had decided, again in winter, again eating dinner on a Sunday night, not to let it pass as though it were any other day, any set of two numerals on the calendar, but to gather, either at home or wherever she and Cal chose to be in the middle of July.

She left the bed, and by that simple motion of pushing away sheet and summer blanket and swinging her feet to the floor, her breath and heart and muscles eased, and softly she left the bedroom and Cal's slow breathing it held, went down the hall and into the kitchen, everything visible though not distinct in this last of darkness and beginning of light her eyes had adjusted to while in bed she listened to birds and saw the fins of sharks.

She still did, standing at the sink in her white gown and looking through the window screen at dark pines, and she heard the mate's scream just after he tied the knot lashing together the two orange life preservers and she had looked up from buckling her life jacket, looked at his scream and saw a face she had never seen before and now would always see: his eyes and mouth widened in final horror and the absolute loss of hope that caused it; then he was gone, as though propelled downward, and his orange life jacket he had waited to put on, had held by one strap in his teeth as he wrapped the line down through the water and up over the sides of the life preservers, floated on the calm blue surface. She saw, too, in her memory that moved into the space of lawn and gray air between her and the pines, the young blond captain bobbing in his jacket in the churning water beneath the helicopter blades. He helped Gina first onto the ladder; Rusty, holding the swinging ropes, watched Gina's legs climbing fast, above the water, glistening brown in the sun; then the captain lifted Rusty and pushed her legs to the rung they were reaching for, and then Ryan and then Cal, and Cal's wet hair blew down and out from his head. Rusty was aboard then, on her hands and knees on the vibrating deck of the helicopter, calling louder, it seemed, than the engine, calling to Cal to hurry, hurry, climb; then she saw the shark's fin and in front of it the rising back and head, its blank and staring eyes, then its mouth as the captain reached for the ladder, but only his left arm rose as she screamed his name so loudly that she did not hear the engine but heard the bite as she saw it and blood spurting into the air, onto the roiled water while the captain's right shoulder still moved upward as though it or the captain still believed it was attached to an arm.

Cal heard her scream. He looked down over his shoulder, then sprang backward into the water, and then she could not scream, or hear the engine, or feel the deck's quick throb against her knees and palms; she could only see Cal's feet hit the water and his legs sink into it, and his body to his ribs before the jacket stopped and lifted him, one arm straight upward, his hand gripping a rung and pulling his arm bent as with the other he reached underwater and pushed the captain up and held him while the captain moved his left hand up the vertical rope to the next rung. Then Cal lifted him again and the captain's feet were on the ladder and she could see Cal's hand pushing his buttocks, and the captain's hand moved up to the next rung and pulled, the sunburn gone now from his face more pale than his sun-bleached hair, and blood fell on Cal and spurted on the water where a fin came with the insouciant speed of nature and her remorseless killing. Cal was looking only at the captain's back above him; he bent one leg out of the water, its thigh pressing his abdomen; then his foot was on the ladder; he straightened his leg and the other ascended from the water as quickly it seemed as it had entered when he jumped over the captain, into the sea. Below him the eyes and head rose from blown waves, then went under, and the fin circled the bound orange preservers turning and rocking and rising and falling in the water and downward rush of air from the huge blades. Their loud circling above her made Rusty feel contained from all other time and space save these moments and feet of rope that both separated her from Cal and joined her to him.

Then quickly and firmly, yet not roughly, a man removed her from the hatch—pushed her maybe; lifted and set her down maybe—and went backward down the ladder. She crawled to the hatch's side: Cal stood behind the captain, his head near the middle of the captain's back, his right hand holding the vertical rope beneath the slowing spurt of blood, his left pulling captain's hand from a rung, pushing it to the one above; then the man descending stopped and held on to the swinging ladder with the crook of his elbow, and hung out above the water and the fins—four now, five—and lowered a white line she had not seen to Cal, then tied it around his waist and held the captain's wrist while Cal circled and knotted the line beneath the orange jacket and the face that now was so white, she knew the captain would die. But her heart did not; it urged the three men up as Cal, with his body, held the captain on the ladder and pushed his hand up to a rung, then lifted his left leg to one, then his right, and followed him up while the crewman, with the line around his waist, slowly climbed until he reached the hatch and leaned through it, his chest on the deck, and Gina and Ryan each took an arm and pulled, and Rusty worked her hands under his web belt at his back, and on her knees she pulled until he was inside, kneeling, then standing and turning seaward, to look down the ladder and tighten the rope and say to any of them behind him: "First-aid kit."

Hand over hand he pulled the rope, looking down the ladder at his work, keeping his pull steady but slow, too, holding the captain on the ladder and between it and Cal. Then at the bottom edge of the hatch, against a background of blue sky and water, the captain's face appeared; then the jacket, and the shoulder she could not look away from but she saw the other one, too, and his left arm that did not reach into the helicopter but simply fell forward and lay still. The crewman stepped back, leaning against the rope around his waist, pulling it faster now but smoothly, and though she could not see Cal, she saw the effort of his push as the captain rose and dropped to the deck. She bent over his back, gripped his belt at both sides, and threw herself backward, and he slid forward as she fell on her rump and sat beside him, on the spot where his right arm would have been, and she felt his blood through her wet jeans. The blood did not spurt now. It flowed, and Cal was aboard, crawling in it, before Rusty or Gina or Ryan could move around the captain to hold out a hand; blood was in Cal's dark brown hair, flecks and smears among the gray streaks and the gray above his ears and in his short sideburns, and on his hands and sleeves and jacket and face. But what Rusty saw in a grateful instant that released her into time and space again was his own blood, pumping within his body, coloring his face a deep, living red.

The helicopter veered and climbed and turned and the crewman rolled the captain onto his back and, without looking, reached up for the compress Gina had removed from the first-aid kit. Rusty looked at her hand, holding the compress as limply as with guilt, then Rusty looked up at the tearless futility of her daughter's face. The compress did not change hands. The crewman was looking at the captain's face and reaching toward Gina's hand; then he lowered his arm and placed his fingers on the captain's throat. Rusty knew from the crewman's eyes, and from the captain's face while he was still on the ladder, that this touch of the pulse was no more than a gesture, like the professionally solemn closing of a casket before its travel from the funeral home to the church service. Her legs lay straight in front of her, and she bent them and with her palms she pushed herself up, stumbling into the imbalance of the helicopter's flight, rising from the captain's blood and wiping it from her palms onto the legs of her jeans.

"And it was his own fault," she said at the kitchen sink, surprised that she had spoken aloud, in a voice softly hoarse, after the silence of sleep. She cleared her throat, but it was dry, so she left the sink and the window and the images between her and the pines of the dead captain in the helicopter, and the first fin—the second: no one had seen the shark that came up under the mate—and poured a glass of orange juice and drank it in one long swallow, her hand still holding open the refrigerator door. She stood looking at the turkey, covered with plastic wrapping, the pan holding it set parallel to the length of the shelf. Last night she had removed the shelf above it to make room for the turkey's breast. She had put in the ice chest the random assortment of food from the shelf that leaned now against one side of the refrigerator. Some of the food she had thrown away—a peach and two oranges molding at the rear of the shelf, a tomato so soft her fingers pierced it, some leaves of rusted lettuce, and a plastic container of tuna fish salad she had made last week—and was angry again at her incompetence, after all these years, at maintaining order in a refrigerator, at even knowing what on a given day it contained. She gazed at the turkey and saw Gina's long bare legs beside hers in the water, bending and then kicking the soles of her sneakers against the noses of sharks.

It was what the captain had told them to do—had shouted at them to do—and for forty-seven minutes, according to the Coast Guard, Rusty had kicked. Her arms were behind her, down through the life preserver, her hands underwater holding the bottom of its rim, which she squeezed against her back. Gina, holding the same preserver, was to her right. Rusty could glance to her left and see Cal's back, his head, and his arms going down through that preserver; Ryan and the captain were behind her. She wore jeans, tight and heavy with water, and when a fin came toward her she drew in her legs, then kicked between the eyes as they surfaced, those eyes that seemed to want her without seeing her. Later when she told the story to friends at home, she said the eyes were like those of an utterly drunken man trying to pick you up in a bar: all but a glimmer of sentience and motive invisible beneath the glaze of drunkenness, so that he did not truly see you, but only woman, bar, night. Those were the men, she told her friends, that even Cal handled gently, saying they were not responsible for anything they said or did. Each time she kicked, and while she readied herself for the next shark, she waited for her blue-jeaned legs to disappear in a crunch and tearing of teeth through her flesh and bones. But more than her own legs she had watched Gina's, or had been aware of them as though she never stopped watching, for while her memory was of Gina's legs and her waiting to see them severed, memory told her, too, that she could not have looked at them as often or for as long as she believed. She had to watch the water in front of her; even to hope for a fin there, because she waited, too, for a shark to come straight up beneath her, to kill her before she even saw it, kicked it. So she had glimpsed Gina's legs, had sometimes looked directly at them when Gina kicked and kicked until the shark turned; but always she had felt those legs, more even than her own; and she had not felt—or had she? and would she ever know?—Cal's legs or body, or Ryan's, though she had called to them, every minute, or so it seemed now: *Cal? Are you all right? Ryan?* She had not felt the captain at all.

She closed the refrigerator, thought of making coffee and starting this day. But it was too early. She wanted the day to be over, wanted tomorrow to come, Monday, the day that since she was a little girl and went for the first time to school, not even school yet but kindergarten, had asserted itself on her life, as an end to weekends, an affirmation of their transitory ease. The turkey held for her now no expectancy: it was only a dead fowl, plucked of its feathers, ugly. She was too cool, and the linoleum floor chilled her bare feet. She went quietly to the bedroom, stood on its carpet, and looked once with loving envy, nearly pride, at Cal sleeping; then she stepped into her slippers and put on her summer robe and dropped her cigarettes and lighter into a pocket, and went out into the hall, where on the wood floor the skidding and slapping sound of her slippers made her halt and for an instant hold her breath. Then lifting and lowering her feet in a slow creeping walk, she went to the bathroom, knowing for the first time since the day woke her that she wanted Cal asleep; she wanted to be alone. She eased open the medicine cabinet and lowered a sleeping pill into the pocket of her robe.

In the kitchen she filled a glass with ice from the chest that held beer, jarred food, and a carton of milk, and pulled a Coke from under ice, and went through the living room and unlatched the screen door. The wooden door had been swung open all night. At home they had an alarm system that four times in three years had frightened away housebreakers. She sat on the old porch swing hanging by chains from the ceiling and looked at the lake, sixty-five feet from the cabin, the owner had said; in the faint light it was dark blue and smooth. On both sides of her were trees, so she could not see the cabins that flanked theirs nor, at this hour, hear the voices and music that later would come through the woods, and around them, too, as though carried by the lake's surface. The lake was very large and around its perimeter were cabins, houses, wharves, boat landings, all separated by woods. Most of the trees were old pines, tall and straight and durable; far across the lake, they were absolutely still, piercing the windless morning light. She poured Coke fizzing over ice and when the foam settled she poured again. She pinched the pill out of her pocket, blew off aqua lint; then, holding it at her mouth, she paused. She would sleep till noon. Then she placed it on her tongue and drank.

Soon she would feel it: the dullness in her legs and arms and behind her eyes, so they would see then only what they looked at, objects and doors and rooms and hall; free of sharks and blood, they would steer her to bed, where she would wake a second time to the fourteenth of July, a day in history she had memorized in school; but a year ago, in a sea as tranquil as this lake, that date had molted the prison and the revolution. As when Vietnam had disappeared in 1968, burned up in Gina's fever when she was nine and had pneumonia. Then Rusty's passive sorrow and anger about the war, harder to bear because they were passive, so on some nights awake in bed she saw herself pouring her blood on draft files, going to jail; and all the pictures of the war her heart received from television and newspapers and magazines; and her imagined visions of the wounded and dying, and the suffering of those alive, first the Vietnamese children, then all Vietnamese and those American boys who were lost in false fervor or drafted and forced to be soldiers so they could survive—all were cold ashes in her mind and heart while for three days Gina, her firstborn, lay on the hospital bed with a needle in her vein and every six hours a nurse added an antibiotic to the fluid, and every four took Gina's temperature. Rusty stayed in the room, watched Gina, read, fell asleep in the chair, ate at the hospital cafeteria; when Cal got home from work he and Ryan came and sat with Gina, while Rusty went home to shower and change clothes, then she returned to spend the night sleeping in the leather armchair. There was no extra bed for her, but two orderlies carried in the larger chair from the sunporch.

On the fourth day Gina's fever was down and Rusty brought her home, to her bed with fresh sheets Rusty had tucked and folded, and for the next ten days she ministered to her, gave her the medicine Gina could swallow now, sat and talked with her, gave her socks and slippers and helped her into her robe when Gina wanted to watch television from the living room couch, where she lay on her side and Rusty covered her with a blanket and sat at the couch's end, with Gina's feet touching her leg, and did not smoke. For those ten days the foolishness Gina watched was not foolishness; their watching it was ceremonial. During these days Rusty's life drew her back into it: she became married again, she cooked meals, and received the praise of Cal and Ryan, who gave it to her by joking about their cereal and sandwiches and Chinese dinners while she was at the hospital. Three times she and Cal made love, and she guided him to long tenderness before she opened herself to him, and did not tell him that his lover's slow kissing and touching were exorcising the vapor of death above their bed, stirring her passion until it consumed her, and left no space in the room or bed or her body for the death of Gina. She did not tell him this because she did not know it herself until months later, and by then she did not want to remember it with him through words, for their sound in her throat would become tears she had already wept at the hospital those three days and three nights when she could not place herself in 1968, could not convince herself that she was living in the age of cures, and that Gina would not die. The word *pneumonia* came to her as though she and Gina lived in 1868, sped at her with the force of a century behind it and struck her breast with a fear she knew but could not feel she ought to reserve for leukemia or some other death knell. As Gina became strong and cheerful and finally restless, the Vietnam War seeped into Rusty's days and nights and she began reading the *Boston Globe* again and watching the news on television, and within the first week of Gina's return to school, her old thwarted sorrow and anger distracted her quietude, and rose in her conversations with her friends and her family.

She felt the pill in her legs now, and in her fingers as she lit her last cigarette before the walk she would have to control to the bedroom. Near the shore in front of the house a mallard swam. In the still air the lake was as calm as the Caribbean on Bastille Day when they fished for marlin. As they headed out to sea in the thirty-two-foot wooden boat, Gina had said: "Let them eat hooks." Rusty killed fish every summer and sometimes, with Cal, pheasants in the fall; the birds were harder to find and she and Cal hunted some seasons without seeing one, save those they refused to shoot on their land; but she loved anyway walking alertly in the cool air and sunlight. When she did shoot a pheasant, she ran before its sun-brightened green hit the earth, ran with her thumb pressing the shotgun's safety button, silently telling the bird: *Don't just be wounded and crawl off to hide and die.* She had given up trying to explain to her friends who did not hunt, both women and men, the thrill of the flushing bird and her gun coming to her shoulder and its muzzle and bead sight swinging up to the shape and colors, the thrill of firing only once and seeing it fall, and her fear as she ran to it, and, above all, the third feeling: sacredness, a joy subdued by sorrow not for the dead bird, or even for her killing it, but for something she knew in her heart yet could not name, something universal and as old as the earth and the first breath of plants. Those same friends who did not understand her hunting were puzzled when she told them that catching even a mackerel, small and plentiful as they were, or a cod that she reeled up from the bottom of the sea onto boats they chartered in New Hampshire, gave her that same feeling when she unhooked them and placed them in the ice chest. She never mentioned to these friends what she felt when she caught a bluefish. It fought as if it were a heavy cod with the vigor of a mackerel, and the fish's struggle for life wearied her right arm and shot through her body, which she leaned backward, then moved forward as she reeled. When she brought it alongside and Cal or Gina or Ryan gaffed it and lifted it onto the deck, she put on thick cotton working gloves and pushed one hand into a gill while with pliers in the other she pulled and twisted and worked out the hook, watching the eye looking at hers and telling her as clearly as if it were human: *I'm going to bite off your finger, you bitch.* She had never shot any game but pheasants or an occasional rabbit, had never caught anything larger than a bluefish; cod had been longer and heavier, but their dead weight on her line, their easy giving up of the hook so she used neither gloves nor pliers, diminished by pounds and inches their size, and kept the fierce bluefish larger in her heart. She did not know whether or not she wanted to catch a marlin; she did not know whether she wanted any of her family to. So when Gina made the joke about hooks, Rusty had quickly turned to her, a scolding sentence taking shape; but she said nothing. For Gina, seeing Rusty's face, had blushed and said: "I just remembered what day it is. That's all." Ryan stepped beside Gina at the gunwale and kissed her cheek and said: "Aristocrat. Or maybe a royal asshole." Cal said: "Did somebody call?"

An hour or two later, some time before noon, the boat sank. It struck nothing. The engine stopped, but there was no sound of wooden bow or hull hitting a reef or upturned sunken boat or a whale. There was no shock, no force to make them fall to the deck or to lurch and reach for one another's bodies for balance. There was only the captain's voice: not even a cry, but a low, clear sentence so weighted with the absolute knowledge of what had happened that to Rusty it was more frightening than a scream, and she saw her long red hair wavering like flame above her as she sank beneath her last bubbles of air: "We have to go overboard; she's sinking." Then he said to the mate, Zack Chaffee, dark and small and muscular, already running forward the few strides from stern to forecastle, and minutes away from his own death: "Get the preservers and jackets." Rusty went forward, too, and felt her family behind and beside her as she halted midway to the forecastle and looked at the water rising in it, covering the bunks. A cushion and two life jackets floated. Chaffee went down the ladder and was in water to his waist. He tossed the two floating jackets out to the deck and saw Rusty and her family, and he was looking at her face when he waved his arm toward the boat's port side and either said or mouthed: "Go." Cal picked up the jackets and gave them to Gina and Ryan, then took her arm and led her to the side. As he lifted her to the gunwale, she heard the captain's voice repeating MAYDAY and the digits of their location and she looked over her shoulder at him before she jumped. Then all of them were in the water, swimming away from the boat, Zack pushing the preservers in front of him, holding his jacket's strap in his teeth, a coil of line around one shoulder; and the captain rising in the water to throw jackets ahead of her and Cal.

Holding a preserver while Zack lashed them, she watched the boat sinking, then looked past Zack at the captain's profile and saw what his first knowledge had been, what she had heard in his voice when he spoke to them on the boat: not of drowning; they were floating and already help was coming from everywhere within range of his radio. He had known why they were sinking, and she knew it was something he had done or had not done, and it should not have happened, should not have been allowed to happen, and she was about to accuse him but could not, for his face was like that of landed codfish, resigned to sunlight and air and death, as if they accepted that they had destroyed themselves, feeding on the dark bottom, taking the clam and the barb with it, and that was why they fought so little, if at all, while she reeled them up, why they were simply weight on the end of her line. The captain's name was Lenny Walters. Watching his face with its look of being caught in a trap that he had set, she forgave him. He looked at his boat until it was gone, and still he stared at the water where it had been as if the gentle waves were a chorus, their peaceful sound of moving water coming to his ears as hue and cry. In the water beside her, Gina and Ryan, twenty-five and twenty-three then, were building a bridge of jokes and laughter over their fear. Cal was asking Zack, but quietly, what the Goddamn hell had happened. Zack was silently tying together the preservers. Rusty looked at his face lowered over the knot, but lowered as well from Cal's voice and eyes. So he knew, too. She looked up at the sky for respite, then pushed her arms through the holes in her life jacket and looked down to buckle the straps, and Zack screamed.

"We can never know for sure," the Coast Guard lieutenant had said. "But that's the only thing that makes sense. I've got four intelligent adults here. And they tell me you were all a lot calmer than people ought to have to be. With what you went through. No panic. Working together in the water, even this fellow"—he nodded toward Cal, smoking in a chair near a window—"going back in to help the captain up when he got it. So I believe the boat didn't hit anything. So I'm going to report that, in my professional opinion, that's exactly what it was. And I want to thank all of you for your time and your courtesy. There's not one thousandth of one percent of the whole human race that's been through what you good people did." He paused. "Not on a fishing trip, anyway. It was probably the first shark that brought the rest, got them feeding. And most times that first shark wouldn't have hit, either. By and large, they're just big fish that leave people alone. So you had a whole lot of bad luck, and a whole lot of good luck to get out of it alive. If there's anything I can do—" But Rusty said: "It wasn't bad luck."

He turned to her, placed his arms on the desk, and leaned over them.

"Beg pardon?" he said. He was a tall man, not broad, and his stomach was widening, would in years to come grow round in front and sag over his khaki belt. Lenny Walters was a very large man, not tall and not fat, but strong; she had only noticed his size when she watched Cal pushing him up the ladder and holding him on it and then the crewman climbing against the pull of the rope around his waist, and at the end when she had gripped Lenny Walters's belt and thrown herself backward onto the deck. Cal was five feet eight inches tall and weighed a hundred and sixty-five pounds, three inches taller and thirty pounds heavier than she, yet for thirty-five years she had seen him as bigger and stronger than everything she feared. Maybe she had not seen the two hundred–odd pounds of Lenny Walters until he was dying on the ladder, because there was something about him that was small, indolent.

"It wasn't bad luck," she said. "The sharks, yes. But not the boat sinking. It wasn't an accident, either. Accidents happen to you. Maybe the first shark was an accident. Maybe he didn't even want Zack. Maybe he wanted something better."

The lieutenant's blue eyes did not move from hers, and they were not distracted, and they were not amused by the unpredictable and mysterious world that so many men believed only women inhabited; they looked at her as one sailor's eyes to another, curious, interested, ready to receive a truth about the unpredictable and mysterious sea they shared. She said: "It was—what's the word?"

"Electrolysis."

"Yes. Of the seacock. He knew. He knew he hadn't

done his maintenance. It was in his voice. When he told us we had to go overboard. I can still hear him. It was in his voice: there was no surprise, you see. Not even excitement. It was like something had been on his mind for a while—"

"A good while," the lieutenant said. "Excuse me."

"—so that brass fitting snapped off and the boat filled under the waterline and he still didn't know it. Then the water burst through the bulkhead into the fo'c'sle and what he had been putting off doing came in on him. And he knew it. It was in his voice, and it was in his face when he was watching his boat go down. It was in Zack's face, too, right up to the moment the shark came."

The lieutenant nodded.

"I believe you," he said. He looked at Cal across the room from Rusty. Cal was watching her. The red in his cheeks deepened. He said: "Maybe that's why he was so good in the water. He was a Goddamned captain in that water. He put Gina up the ladder first. I don't believe he was thinking women and children first, either. He knew there was just us four in the family. I think he picked her first because she can still have babies." Cal's eyes did not shift to Gina, or to Ryan when he said: "Then Ryan. Same reason, I suppose. He can't have them, but he can get them started. Then the mother. Then the old bastard that's paid his dues and his insurance premiums, too. Then the poor son of a bitch paid all his dues at once."

The deeper color was still in his cheeks and she saw in his eyes the dampness of tears he would contain, but his hands did not rise to them, either; he let them glisten there, for her. To her left, Gina sniffled. Still watching Cal, her face warmed by his, she reached to Gina, who with two hands took hers and tightened and stroked and squeezed and stroked, and Rusty saw those lovely brown legs in the blue water. Had a shark's jaws opened for one, she would have triumphantly thrust her own leg into its mouth. Yet Cal, without even a pause to look for another way to get Lenny Walters onto the ladder, had leaped backward into the sea, among the sharks whose number they would never know. Looking at him across the small room, she felt no shame or envy. She saw only Cal, and in his face she saw only herself, and though she felt the chair she sat in, and Gina's hands moving on hers, she felt bodiless, too, out of the room, as though her spirit and Cal's had left their bodies and were moving side by side, above time, above mortality. Then she was in her body again, in the room and the cool of the trade winds coming through the window behind Cal, and she was aware again of the tall lieutenant. She looked at him, then at Ryan, then at Gina. They were all watching her, as they might if she had beautifully sung an aria, and they could not yet speak, suspended in that instant of purity before their hands would move to clap and their legs would push them out of their chairs to their feet.

On the porch swing she carefully lowered the glass with its melting ice to the floor. She had a few minutes still to sit and watch the lake, time even for another cigarette, though her fingers were slow and heavy with it, and her mind was moving back through the house, into bed and sleep, its path cluttered with images it tried to skirt: a large codfish staring straight ahead at air as she gently removed the hook; a bluefish pressed down by her knee, flopping and twisting against her gloved hand in its gill, biting the shank of the hook and glaring at her; the strange eyes of sharks driven from feeding by kicking feet. But the pill neither distorted nor quieted her heart. Its beat was not as rapid as when it woke her; but it was strong, so eager now for the day that she was glad she had taken the pill, for excitement would have kept her awake as it does a child.

She saw motion to her right: not a thing or a creature, but only its movement. She sat very still, moved her eyes toward it, and saw a doe drinking at the lake: she stood on earth darkened by pines in the twilight, her graceful and exposed neck lowered to the water. She was no more than a hundred feet away. Then Rusty saw motion again, and behind the doe, at the edge of the woods, the antlers and head and shoulders of a buck seemed to separate themselves from the trees. Then it stopped. Quietly Rusty breathed the smell of pines and water. The chains of the swing creaked and seemed very loud to her, as the beating of her heart seemed audible to the ears beneath the antlers. But the buck did not move, and the doe lapped water, and Rusty wanted to hear that sound but could not. The buck lifted its head. Then he stepped forward once, swung his head in an arc that started up the lake and ended with her. She stared at his nose and eyes and antlers, and did not move. He looked at the doe backing away from the water, raising her head; then Rusty saw the length of his body emerge from the woods, as if it were growing out of the trees, just fast enough for her to see. At the lake he stopped, his head up, listening. Then he drank. Rusty tossed her cigarette to the lawn and watched him drinking, and the doe turning back to the woods, then disappearing into it. She waited until the buck finished drinking and vanished, too.

She pushed herself up from the swing and at the sound of its chains she stopped and listened for the running deer, but heard only water lapping at the shore. She had not been drunk for over ten years, and in her sleepy happiness she smiled at her walk through the cabin, no more than two steps in a straight line before she swerved, slowly and heavily, and in the hall to the bedroom she kept her palms on both walls till she reached the door and Cal's breathing. She stood in the doorway, aiming herself at the bed and her side of it, the far side. Then she moved, weaving, her arms up and out for balance. *Like dancing,* she thought, and felt like twirling but knew she would fall. When she turned the corner of the foot of the bed, she did fall: she simply let go all control of herself and landed on the mattress and laughed with a sound as soft as Cal's breath. He rolled toward her, then opened his eyes. They were calm, like Gina's and Ryan's were when they quietly woke in their cradles, then cribs on mornings when they were neither hungry nor uncomfortably wet, only awake. She kissed both of his eyes shut and with her thickened tongue said: "I took a pill. But wake me up anyway. With coffee. Okay?"

"A pill," he said as sleep drew him away from her. Then he opened his eyes. "Why?"

"I couldn't sleep."

"I know. But why?"

"Today."

Her eyes closed and she was asleep but trying to return, and she forced open her lids.

"I was on the porch. Remembering all of it. You."
She laid her hand on his side, pressed his ribs. "It was
the worst day our family's ever had."

"It was the worst day most families have ever had."

Her eyes closed.

"But it was the best, too," she said, her voice de-
tached from her body, coming from a throat somewhere above her. She felt his voice close to her face, but
she heard one word at a time, then it drifted away from
her, and the next word and the next were alone, and
meant nothing.

"Do you understand?" she said.

Then his mouth was at her ear, and she heard: "I
said yes."

"Good. Make the coffee strong."

His hand was smoothing her hair back from her
forehead; he was talking, and his voice was gentle. She
heard only her name, then was asleep.

Sunday Morning

O N A S U N D A Y M O R N I N G I N S U M M E R , I N A
brass bed, a woman lay awake and naked with
her new lover. He was asleep and was on his left side,
facing her; the yellow sheet covered him to his waist.
She was on her back and had pulled the sheet over her
breasts. Her skin and brown hair were dark. He had a
hairy chest and light brown hair, his suntan was tinged
with pink, and she could see the night's growth of
whiskers on his face. During the night she had raised
the venetian blinds at the window on his side of the
bed. She lived on the second floor and the window
faced north, above a courtyard. The bed was still in
shadow; opposite its foot, the white wall and a framed
poster were in sunlight. The poster was a colored pho-

tograph of a ballerina's legs, in black tights and leg warmers, her pink-slippered feet standing on pointe.

The woman's name was Tess, and she was thirty-six years old. In her twenties and early thirties she had made love with more men than she had loved. But sometime after her thirty-fifth birthday she became suddenly afraid that she would never have children, and that when her beauty aged she would grow old and die alone, and she began waiting for a husband. Her fear could not have been that sudden, but in memory it seemed so, as if she had waked to it one ordinary morning. The new lover was her third since that fear had come into her life. She met the second in January, and he was gone by April. She knew she had frightened him: he was her age, and was in no hurry to have children. The first was her boyfriend for nearly a year, but he cheated on her; when she gathered the courage to know it, she broke up with him in one angry and cathartic hour, the two of them standing with drinks in her kitchen. They both lived in Boston and she was afraid she would see him one night, with another woman, but she did not see him again after yelling at him everything she believed he was and was not.

Now she watched her lover's sleeping face. His name was Andrew; he was thirty-seven and had never married. She met him in a supermarket, and on their first date he told her he had been hoping for some time to meet a woman in the supermarket; he had looked at ring fingers and the contents of shopping carts to see who might be living alone. Friends had arranged dates for him, but they didn't come to anything, and he felt he was too old to meet women in bars; he wanted something different now, something more stable. She did not ask him what he meant. Once while they were eating dinner in a restaurant she watched his eyes as she told him she would like someday to have a child; maybe two. He had blue eyes. They were what drew her to him in the supermarket; they were what made her reply when he spoke to her while they were choosing oranges. Across the dinner table, when she talked of a child, his eyes did not shift or become guarded; they looked brightly at her over the candle flame. Sometimes she believed their light came from images of marrying her and fathering children, and other times she believed it was simply lust, and that she could have been telling him that she wanted someday to take up golf.

She knew her bitterness was real, earned over the years of indulging herself, and she must not do that anymore, nor allow anyone to do it with her. She held Andrew at bay for four weeks. But he was so sweet, so good to her, and last night she took again the old risk of having him too quickly, so losing him too soon: when he followed her into the apartment for a nightcap, she turned on him with a long kiss and embrace that lasted while she backed down the hall and into her bedroom and unbuckled his belt and unzipped and pulled his pants free of his hips. Now she would not be able to keep him out of her bed again, and she would not want to, and she wished that in the month since they went side by side from the fruit and vegetables through the rest of the store, he had said he wanted children or had at least noticed cute ones in the city or at the beach. She wanted him awake, so she got up and brushed her teeth and made coffee, and when she came back to bed, carrying the cups, he was in the bathroom. She placed the cups on the one bedside table; it was brown wood, and on it were a clock radio and a shaded lamp. Once in the night, while making love, she had switched on the light and watched Andrew's face. She sat in bed now and pulled the sheet over her lap. She heard his light steps in the hall and watched the doorway to see him walk in naked. She looked at all of him she could see and he smiled. When he sat on the bed, she gave him his coffee and said: "Do you like it in the morning the way you like it after dinner?"

"Just the same," he said, and kissed her. She tasted toothpaste, and she liked thinking of him using her toothbrush. He sipped the coffee with the cream and one teaspoon of sugar, then put the cup on the table with hers and kissed her and touched her. She was happy to be making love again on a Sunday morning, but something distracted her, and she could not come; when he did, she moaned and moved faster and he believed her. The coffee was still hot enough; they sat up to drink it, and he said: "Do you eat breakfast?"

"Sometimes. Would you like eggs or something? Pancakes?"

"Let me take you out for brunch."

She thought of them coming back from brunch to make love again, to fall asleep in midafternoon, and she saw him going home to his shower and razor and clothes, and the sun setting while she put a frozen dinner in the microwave so she could eat before dark; she saw the last shadows in the courtyard below the kitchen and on the street in front of her apartment; saw herself

driving in dusk to the video store. She wanted a cigarette but she had quit and you could never get one from
a man anymore. He was watching her.

"So," he said. "Are you hungry?"

"Did you ever smoke?"

"No. Did you?"

"I quit at New Year's." She looked away from him,
at the sunlit wall, and drank from her cup. "I had a
friend once. A girlfriend, from college. Mona Baker.
She kept her maiden name when she got married. She
was married for six years, and I swear to God she loved
him the whole time; I'd have known it if she didn't."
She looked at Andrew. "When she was three months
pregnant with their first child, he killed her."

"Jesus. In a fight?"

"No. He never got drunk. He never hit her. You'd
see them together, and you'd think, *That's how a couple
should be.* He watched her when she talked. He actually
listened to her. No: he planned it. And near the end,
while he was planning it, nobody could see anything
different between them. Not even Mona. This was
three years ago." She closed her eyes and in their darkness those three years fell away and she clearly saw
Mona's face and blond hair on the day they'd had
lunch together. She opened her eyes; Andrew was sipping his coffee, watching her over the cup. "You should
have seen him, the proud father-to-be."

"I don't understand somebody like that. Usually it's
passion."

"What is?"

"Homicide. Except with the Mafia. Your friend's
husband was sick."

"He was her husband. They made love. They wanted a child. Or she thought he did."

"Was there another woman?"

"No. He wanted the money."

"What money?"

"The insurance."

"How much?"

"Seven hundred and fifty thousand."

"For what?"

"Who knows? His dreams. She thought she had hers. First they bought a house. Good-bye to apartments." She glanced around the bedroom and saw in her mind the small bathroom, and the kitchen with no space for a table, and the living-and-dining room that faced brick apartments across the street. Sunlight was on the wicker chair now; over its back, her dress from last night lay on Andrew's shirt and pants. "It was a good house in a good neighborhood, an easy drive to Boston. That was one reason they chose it, and the other was the schools." She looked at Andrew. "Can you imagine that? For the schools."

"Did they get him for first-degree?"

"Yes. He's in prison till he dies."

"When he's old, they'll let him out."

"Then maybe somebody in her family will kill him."

"You said her name was Baker." He looked amused, close to smiling.

"What's that mean?"

"Never mind."

"No. What?"

"A joke. Forget it."

"What joke. Tell me."

"I was going to say Baker isn't Italian."

"Maybe you're right. Maybe I should go live in Sicily. Maybe that's where the men are." He touched her arm, but she twisted away. With one long swallow she drank the last of her coffee and put the cup on the table. "Probably they have one Goddamn cigarette for you with your morning coffee."

She looked over the table at the shadowed wall and brown louvered closet door.

"Hey," he said. "Hey, Tess. I'll go get some."

He stroked her back with his palm, and soon she felt only that, his hand on her spine and muscles; then she turned to him and said: "I'm sorry. I loved her so much."

"Is that store on the corner open?"

He reached past her and placed his cup beside hers.

"No. I mean yes, it is, but I don't want to smoke. But thank you." Still his face looked troubled, his body poised. With her left hand she touched his cheek. "Really. Okay?" She watched his face settle. Then she moved her hand to her brow, touched it with her fingertips. "He shot her in the face. Here." She lowered her hand and held the sheet covering her legs. "He used one of those snub-nosed thirty-eights. For a long time I tried not to see movies with guns in them, but that's not easy. I was dating. I didn't want to seem weird. And I'd see those guns on the screen, and I'd see Mona turning to look at him, maybe to smile, maybe to say something, and seeing it pointed at her face. She was in the bedroom. She was in her nightgown, brushing her hair at the mirror. He came in with the gun behind his back. When he confessed, he said he wanted to do it while she was asleep, but there would be blood on the bed. He wanted it to look like they heard a guy in their room and woke up. Like he went for the guy and Mona was going to the phone and the guy pulled out a gun and shot her."

"They didn't have a phone beside the bed?"

"No. They didn't like a phone in the bedroom; they turned off the ringer at night; the upstairs phone was in the hall; they—*Jesus*."

"What?"

"I hate saying 'they.'" She looked at Andrew's face, his eyes calm, lips relaxed, a man listening to a story, her lover right now, maybe her boyfriend, and her thirty-six years of life seemed very long, with too many stories ever to tell to anyone. "He shot her, then knocked a chair over and dumped her jewelry box on the floor. Then he held the gun in his left hand and shot his right shoulder, and put the gun in the toilet tank and called the police. But they saw through his story at the hospital and found the gun."

"There must have been another woman."

"Why do you say that?"

"Seven hundred and fifty thousand dollars isn't enough. Not to kill for."

"And love is?"

"Nothing is. I'm only thinking a combination of the two might work on somebody. If he's sick to begin with."

"Well there wasn't. He wanted to buy a fucking nightclub."

His eyebrows arched as he smiled.

"I've never heard you say that."

"You did last night."

He lowered his eyes while a brief and faint blush colored the skin beneath them. Then it was gone, and he looked at her again.

"He didn't want to be married anymore. He wanted money, then sure, other women. But he didn't have one yet. I keep seeing her face. Turning from the mirror. She probably saw him in the mirror. And she turned and he pointed the gun and then that would be what she saw. The hole of the barrel. And his face above it. I just keep seeing her." She heard tears in her voice, but she kept them from her eyes. "And I see her one other time. One day when we had lunch." She closed her eyes and saw the small table with the white cloth, and the glasses of Burgundy and bowls of green pea soup, and Mona in a blue sweater. "She had seventeen days and sixteen nights to live. We were eating soup, and she was telling me he had taken out more life insurance. On each of them. She was telling me this, like you tell anything that's casual, that just comes to your mind, and she was bringing the spoon to her mouth, just like this—" She moved her right hand, shaped to hold a spoon, up level with her breasts and stopped it there. "Then she said: 'I don't know why he's taking out so much insurance on me.' And she held the spoon there for a moment, looking at me. Then she waved her left hand past her eyes, just once. Like she was fanning smoke away from them. Then she brought her spoon to her mouth, and I don't remember saying anything or even thinking anything; maybe I said because of the baby, maybe I thought it, I don't know. Who does? Who knows anything? We started talking about something else, and there it was, there was the truth, there and gone. Is that what she was pushing away? If she had just held the spoon or put it back in the bowl, if she had just frozen in her chair and really looked very closely right in front of her eyes. Do you think she could have seen it?" He was shaking his head, and she saw the wariness in his eyes, but she could not stop. "Is that what happens? We lie and lie to ourselves till we can't even know our husband doesn't love us anymore, can't even know he hates us, he wants us dead dead dead in the ground, he wants to kill us, never mind we made a baby with him, never mind we're carrying the baby, never mind how much we fucked him and sucked him and looked pretty for him, you probably didn't hear me say love last night either, I certainly didn't hear you say it, I know, I know, it's my fault for—"

She could not look at his eyes anymore, so she closed hers. He was not touching her, but his smells and weight and movements on the mattress surrounded her; yet at the same time she felt enclosed by something as blank as air but solid. She lowered her chin to her breastbone, and she slowed her breathing, and saw and heard what she wanted this morning with Andrew: he walked in naked from the bathroom and said: *Good morning,* and she said: *Good morning, did you sleep well?* and he said: *Yes,* and got into bed, and she handed him the cup of coffee and he sipped it and said: *Perfect,* and said: *How are you?* and she said: *Fine, and you?* He said: *Good. It's a beautiful day,* and she said: *When the wind is blowing from the east, you can smell the ocean,* and he said: *There's no wind today,* and she said: *No, and it feels humid; it'll be hot,* and he said: *Maybe we'll get some rain.*

She opened her eyes. In his she could see flight like birds, flying inward through that lovely blue, down to his heart. Birds that made no sound at all, and she heard his breath and her own, and when he looked away from her, looked straight ahead and bent his knees, she heard the sheets on his legs, and when he placed his folded arms on his knees, she heard the mattress move. She looked at the left side of his face until she heard the air outside her window.

All the Time in the World

IN COLLEGE, LUANN WAS MIRTHFUL AND romantic, an attractive girl with black hair and dark skin and eyes. She majored in American Studies, and her discipline kept her on the dean's list. Her last name was Arceneaux; her mother's maiden name was Voorhies, and both families had come to Maine from Canada. Her parents and sister and brother and LuAnn often gestured with their hands as they talked. Old relatives in Canada spoke French.

LuAnn's college years seemed a fulfillment of her adolescence; she lived with impunity in a dormitory in Boston, with both girls and boys, with drinking and marijuana and cocaine; at the same time, she remained under the aegis of her parents. They were in a small town three hours north by bus; she went there on a few weekends, and during school vacations, and in summer. She was the middle child, between a married sister and a brother in high school. Her parents were proud of her work, they enjoyed her company, and they knew or pretended they knew as little about her life with friends as they had when she lived at home and walked a mile to school. In summer during college she was a lifeguard at a lake with a public beach. She saved some money and her parents paid her tuition and gave her a small allowance when she lived in the dormitory. They were neither strict nor lenient; they trusted her and, at home, she was like a young woman of their own generation: she drank and smoked with them, and on Sundays went to Mass with them and her brother. She went to Sunday Mass in Boston, too, and sometimes at noon on weekdays in the university chapel, and sitting in the pew she felt she was at home: that here, among strangers, she was all of herself, and only herself, forgiven and loved.

This was a time in America when courting had given way to passion, and passion burned without vision; this led to much postcoital intimacy, people revealing themselves to each other after they were lovers, and often they were frightened or appalled by what they heard as they were lying naked on a bed. Passion became smoke and left burned grass and earth on the sheets. The couple put on their clothes, fought for a few months, or tried with sincere and confessional negotiation to bring back love's blinding heat, then parted from each other and waited for someone else. While LuAnn was in college, she did not understand all of this, though she was beginning to, and she did not expect her parents to understand any of it. She secretly took birth control pills and, when she was at home, returned from dates early enough to keep at bay her parents' fears. At Mass she received Communion, her conscience set free by the mores of her contemporaries and the efficacy of the pill. When her parents spoke of drugs and promiscuity among young people, she turned to them an innocent face. This period of enjoying adult pleasures and at times suffering their results, while still living with her parents as a grown child, would end with the commencement she yearned for, strove for, and dreaded.

When it came, she found an apartment in Boston and a job with an insurance company. She worked in public relations. June that year was lovely, and some days she took a sandwich and cookies and fruit to work, and ate lunch at the Public Garden so she could sit in the sun among trees and grass. For the first time in her life she wore a dress or skirt and blouse five days a week, and this alone made her feel that she had indeed graduated to adult life. So did the work: she was assistant to a woman in her forties, and she liked the woman and learned quickly. She liked having an office and a desk with a telephone and typewriter on it. She was proud of her use of the telephone. Until now a telephone had been something she held while talking with friends and lovers and her family. At work she called people she did not know and spoke clearly in a low voice.

The office was large, with many women and men at desks, and she learned their names, and presented to them an amiability she assumed upon entering the building. Often she felt that her smiles, and her feigned interest in people's anecdotes about commuting and complaints about colds, were an implicit and draining part of her job. A decade later she would know that spending time with people and being unable either to speak from her heart or to listen with it was an imperceptible bleeding of her spirit.

Always in the office she felt that she was two people at once. She believed that the one who performed at the desk and chatted with other workers was the woman she would become as she matured, and the one she concealed was a girl destined to atrophy, and become a memory. The woman LuAnn worked for was an intense, voluble blonde who colored her hair and was cynical, humorous, and twice-divorced. When she spoke of money, it was with love, even passion; LuAnn saw money as currency to buy things with and pay bills, not an acquisition to accumulate and compound, and she felt like a lamb among wolves. The woman had a lover, and seemed happy.

LuAnn appreciated the practical function of insurance and bought a small policy on her own life, naming her parents as beneficiaries; she considered it a partial payment of her first child's tuition. But after nearly a year with the insurance company, on a Saturday afternoon while she was walking in Boston, wearing jeans and boots and a sweatshirt and feeling the sun on her face and hair, she admitted to herself that insurance bored her. Soon she was working for a small publisher. She earned less money but felt she was closer to the light she had sometimes lived in during college, had received from teachers and books and other students and often her own work. Now she was trying to sell literature, the human attempt to make truth palpable and delightful. There was, of course, always talk of money; but here, where only seven people worked and book sales were at best modest, money's end was much like its end in her own life: to keep things going. She was the publicity director and had neither assistants nor a secretary. She worked with energy and was not bored; still, there were times each day when she watched herself, and listened to herself, and the LuAnn Arceneaux she had known all her life wanted to say aloud: *Fuck* this; and to laugh.

She had lovers, one at a time; this had been happening since she was seventeen. After each one, when her sorrow passed and she was again resilient, she hoped for the next love; and her unspoken hope, even to herself, was that her next love would be her true and final one. She needed a name for what she was doing with this succession of men, and what she was doing was not clear. They were not affairs. An affair had a concrete parameter: the absence of all but physical love; or one of the lovers was married; or both of them were; or people from different continents met on a plane flying to a city they would never visit again; something hot and sudden like that. What LuAnn was doing was more complicated, and sometimes she called it naked dating: you went out to dinner, bared your soul and body, and in the morning went home to shower and dress for work. But she needed a word whose connotation was serious and deep, so she used the word everyone else used, and called it a relationship. It was not an engagement, or marriage; it was entered without vows or promises, but existed from one day to the next. Some people who were veterans of many relationships stopped using the word, and said things like: *I'm seeing Harry*, and *Bill and I are fucking*.

The men saw marriage as something that might happen, but not till they were well into their thirties.

One, a tall, blond, curly-haired administrator at the insurance company, spoke of money; he believed a man should not marry until paying bills was no longer a struggle, until he was investing money that would grow and grow, and LuAnn saw money growing like trees, tulips, wild grass and vines. When she loved this man, she deceived herself and believed him. When she no longer loved him, she knew he was lying to her and to himself as well. Money had become a lie to justify his compromise of the tenderness and joy in his soul; these came forth when he was with her. At work he was ambitious and cold, spoke of precedent and the bottom line, and sometimes in the office she had to see him naked in her mind in order to see him at all.

One man she briefly loved, a sound engineer who wrote poems, regarded children as spiteful ingrates, fatherhood as bad for blood pressure, and monogamy as absurd. The other men she loved talked about marriage as a young and untried soldier might talk of war: sometimes they believed they could do it, and survive as well; sometimes they were afraid they could not; but it remained an abstraction that would only become concrete with the call to arms, the sound of drums and horns and marching feet. She knew with each man that the drumroll of pregnancy would terrify him; that even the gentlest—the vegetarian math teacher who would not kill the mice that shared his apartment—would gratefully drive her to an abortion clinic and tenderly hold her hand while she opened her legs. She knew this so deeply in her heart that it was hidden from her; it lay in the dark, along with her knowledge that she would die.

But her flesh knew the truth, and told her that time

and love were in her body, not in a man's brain. In her body a man ejaculated, and the plastic in her uterus allowed him to see time as a line rising into his future, a line his lovemaking would not bend toward the curve of her body, the circle of love and time that was her womb and heart. So she loved from one day to the next, blinded herself to the years ahead, until hope was tired legs climbing a steep hill, until hope could no longer move upward or even stand aching in one flat and solid place. Then words came to her, and she said them to men, with derision, with anger, and with pain so deep that soon she could not say them at all, but only weep and, through the blur of tears, look at her lover's angry and chastened eyes. The last of her lovers before she met her final one was a carpenter with Greek blood, with dark skin she loved to see and touch; one night while they ate dinner in his kitchen, he called commitment "the *c* word." LuAnn was twenty-eight then. She rose from her chair, set down her glass of wine, and contained a scream while she pointed at him and said in a low voice: "You're not a man. You're a boy. You all are. You're all getting milk through the fence. You're a thief. But you don't have balls enough to take the cow."

This was in late winter, and she entered a period of abstinence, which meant that she stopped dating. When men asked her out, she said she needed to be alone for a while, that she was not ready for a relationship. It was not the truth. She wanted love, but she did not want her search for it to begin in someone's bed. She had been reared by both parents to know that concupiscence was at the center of male attention; she learned it soon enough anyway in the arms of frenzied boys. In high school she also learned that her passion was not engendered by a boy, but was part of her, as her blood and spirit were, and then she knew the words and actions she used to keep boys out of her body were also containing her own fire, so it would not spread through her flesh until its time. Knowing its time was not simple, and that is why she stopped dating after leaving the carpenter sitting at his table, glaring at her, his breath fast, his chest puffed with words that did not come soon enough for LuAnn to hear. She walked home on lighted sidewalks with gray snow banked on their curbs, and she did not cry. For months she went to movies and restaurants with women. On several weekends she drove to her parents' house, where going to sleep in her room and waking in it made her see clearly the years she had lived in Boston; made her feel that, since her graduation from college, only time and the age of her body had advanced, while she had stood on one plane, repeating the words and actions she regarded as her life.

On a Sunday morning in summer, she put on a pink dress and white high-heeled shoes and, carrying a purse, walked in warm sunlight to the ten o'clock Mass. The church was large and crowded. She did not know this yet, but she would in her thirties: the hot purity of her passion kept her in the Church. When she loved, she loved with her flesh, and to her it was fitting and right, and did not need absolving by a priest. So she had never abandoned the Eucharist; without it, she felt the Mass, and all of the Church, would be only ideas she could get at home from books; and because of it, she overlooked what was bureaucratic or picayune about the Church. Abortion was none of these; it was in the air like war. She hoped never to conceive a child she did not want, and she could not imagine giving death to a life in her womb. At the time for Communion she stepped into the line of people going to receive the mystery she had loved since childhood. A woman with gray hair was giving the Hosts; she took a white disk from the chalice, held it before her face, and said: "The Body of Christ." LuAnn said: "Amen," and the woman placed it in her palms and LuAnn put it in her mouth and for perhaps six minutes then, walking back to her pew and kneeling, she felt in harmony with the entire and timeless universe. This came to her every Sunday, and never at work; sometimes she could achieve it if she drove out of the city on a sunlit day and walked alone on a trail in woods, or on the shore of a lake.

After Mass she lingered on the church steps till she was alone. Few cars passed, and scattered people walked or jogged on the sidewalk, and a boy on a skateboard clattered by. She descended, sliding her hand down the smooth stone wall. A few paces from the steps, she turned her face up to the sun; then the heel of her left shoe snapped, and her ankle and knee gave way: she gained her balance and raised her foot and removed the broken shoe, then the other one. Her purse in one hand and her shoes in the other, she went to the steps and sat and looked at the heel hanging at an angle from one tiny nail whose mates were bent, silver in the sunlight. A shadow moved over her feet and up her legs and she looked at polished brown loafers and a wooden cane with a shining brass tip, and a man's legs in jeans, then up at his face: he had a trimmed brown beard and blue eyes and was smiling;

his hair was brown and touched the collar of his navy blue shirt. His chest was broad, his waist was thick and bulged over his belt, and his bare arms were large; he said: "I could try to fix it."

"With what?"

He blushed, and said: "It was just a way of talking to you."

"I know."

"Would you like brunch?"

"Will they let me in barefoot?"

"When they see the shoe."

He held out his hand, and she took it and stood; her brow was the height of his chin. They told each other their names; he was Ted Briggs. They walked, and the concrete was warm under her bare feet. She told him he had a pretty cane, and asked him why.

"Artillery, in the war. A place called Khe Sanh."

"I know about Khe Sanh."

He looked at her.

"You do?"

"Yes."

"Good," he said.

"Why?"

"You were very young then."

"So were you."

"Nineteen."

"I was twelve."

"So how do you know about Khe Sanh?"

"I took a couple of courses. It's the best way to go to war."

He smiled, and said: "I believe it."

At a shaded corner they stopped to cross the street

and he held her elbow as she stepped down from the curb. She knew he was doing this because of the filth and broken glass, and that he wanted to touch her, and she liked the feel of his hand. She liked the gentle depth of his voice, and his walk; his right knee appeared inflexible, but he walked smoothly. It was his eyes she loved; she could see sorrow in them, something old he had lived with, and something vibrant and solid, too. She felt motion in him, and she wanted to touch it. He was a lawyer; he liked to read and he liked movies and deep-sea fishing. On their left, cars stopped for a red light; he glanced at her, caught her gazing at his profile, and she said: "It was bad, wasn't it?"

He stopped and looked down at her.

"Yes. I was a corpsman. You know, the nurse, the EMT—" She nodded. "With the Marines. I got hurt in my twelfth month. Ten years later I started dealing with the eleven and a half months before that."

"How's it going?"

"Better. My knee won't bend, but my head is clear in the morning."

They walked; his hand with the cane was close to her left arm, and she could feel the air between their hands and wrists and forearms and biceps, a space with friction in it, and she veered slightly closer so their skin nearly touched. They reached the street where she lived and turned onto it, facing the sun, and she did not tell him this was her street. On the first block was the restaurant; she had walked or driven past it but had not been inside. He held the door for her and she went into the dark cool air and softened lights, the smells of bacon and liquor. She was on a carpet now, and she could see the shapes of people at tables, and hear low voices; then he moved to her right side, lightly placed his hand on her forearm, and guided her to a booth. They ordered: a Bloody Mary for her and orange juice for him, and cantaloupes and omelettes and Canadian bacon with English muffins. When their drinks came, she lit a cigarette and said: "I drink. I smoke. I eat everything."

"I go to meetings. I'm in my sixth year without a drink. My second without smoking." His hand came midway across the table. "But I'd love a hit off yours."

She gave him the cigarette, her fingers sliding under his. She left her hand there, waited for his fingers again, and got them, his knuckles beneath hers, and she paused for a moment before squeezing the cigarette and withdrawing her hand. She said: "Doesn't cheating make you miss it more?"

"Oh, I'm always missing something."

"Drinking?"

"Only being able to. Or thinking I was."

"Nothing horrible has ever happened to me."

"I hope nothing does."

"I suppose if I live long enough something will."

"If you don't live long enough, *that* would be horrible. Are you seeing anyone?"

"No. Are you?"

"No. I'm waiting. I limp. I get frightened suddenly, when there's no reason to be. I get sad too, when nothing has happened. I know its name now, and—"

"What is its name?"

"It. It's just it, and I go about my day or even my week sometimes, then it's gone. The way a fever is

there, and then it isn't. I want a home with love in it,
with a woman and children."

"My God," she said, and smiled, nearly laughing,
her hands moving up from the table. "I don't think I've
ever heard those words from the mouth of a man."

"I love the way you talk with your hands."

They stayed in the booth until midafternoon; he invited her to a movie that night; they stepped out of the
restaurant into the bright heat, and he walked with her
to the door of her apartment building, and stood holding her hand. She raised her bare heels and kissed his
cheek, the hair of his beard soft on her chin, then went
inside. She showered for a long time and washed her
hair and, sitting at her mirror, blew it dry. She put on
a robe and slept for an hour and woke happily. She ate
a sandwich and soup, and dressed and put on makeup.
He lived near the church, and he walked to her building and they walked to the movie; the sun was very low,
and the air was cooling. After the movie he took her
hand and held it for the four blocks to her apartment,
where, standing on the sidewalk, he put his arms
around her, the cane touching her right calf, and they
kissed. She heard passing cars, and people talking as
they walked by; then for a long time she heard only
their lips and tongues, their breath, their moving arms
and hands. Then she stepped away and said: "Not yet."

"That's good."

"You keep saying that."

"I keep meaning it."

He waited until she was inside both doors, and she
turned and waved and he held up his hand till she was
on the elevator, and she waved again as the door closed.

In her apartment she went to her closet and picked up the white shoe with the broken heel. She did not believe in fate, but she believed in gifts that came; they moved with angels and spirits in the air, were perhaps delivered by them. Her red fingernails were lovely on the white leather; her hands warmed the heel.

In the morning she woke before the clock radio started, and made the bed; tonight she would see him. In her joy was fear, too, but it was a good fear of the change coming into her life. It had already come, she knew that; but she would yield slowly to it. She felt her months alone leaving her; she was shedding a condition; it was becoming her past. Outside in the sun, walking to work, she felt she could see the souls of people in their eyes. The office was bright; she could feel air touching her skin, and the warmth of electric lights. With everyone she felt tender and humorous and patient, and happily mad. She worked hard, with good concentration, and felt this, too, molting: this trying to plunder from an empty cave a treasure for her soul. She went to lunch with two women, and ordered a steak and a beer. Her friends were amused; she said she was very hungry, and kept her silence.

What she had now was too precious and flammable to share with anyone. She knew that some night with Ted it would burst and blaze, and it would rise in her again and again, would course in her blood, burn in her face, shine in her eyes. And this time love was taking her into pain, yes, quarrels and loneliness and boiling rage; but this time there was no time, and love was taking her as far as she would go, as long as she would live, taking her strongly and bravely with this Ted Briggs, holding his pretty cane; this man who was frightened by what had happened to him, but not by the madness she knew he was feeling now. She was hungry, and she talked with her friends and waited for her steak, and for all that was coming to her: from her body, from the earth, from radiant angels poised in the air she breathed.

Woman on a Plane

FOR MARIE

SHE WAS IN HER THIRTIES, A POET, AND SHE was afraid to fly. Her brother was dying in another city. She did not have a husband or children, but she had a job that held her in the city where she lived. Until her brother went home to die, her job was work she gave her time to. But now it was taking time from her. She could feel it.

She read poems that students wrote; she read poems in books and in the evenings she lived with them, thought of what she would say about them next day in the classroom. She knew that she could not plan everything she would say; she could only plan how she would begin. It was a matter of letting go in front of the students, and waiting for the light to come. The light would come with images and words she must not hold before class. Her holding them could take away the life they drew from revelation, turn them into dead objects she possessed and carried with her to show the students. She knew that teaching a poem was like writing a poem: she could only begin, and reach, and wait. If she tried to impose a design to save herself from failure, there would be no revelation on the page, or with her students. Before each class she was afraid, but it was muted, and she knew it kept her from being dull and removed. She loved all of this until her brother was dying, and drawing her to him. Then she felt separated from her work, and had to will herself into her voice, into her very flesh.

Grief held her. Always: while she was talking with students, eating with friends, its arms encircled her. Alone, she gave in to it, allowed it to hold her while she fed and cleaned her body, and breathed. It held her when she sat at her desk to do the work that was only for herself; it pressed her biceps to her ribs, her back and breast to her heart, and she could not make a poem grow. She sat with paper and pen and wrote words, but she felt as she did when she drank coffee and ate toast, that she was only doing this because she was alive, and awake. On weekends she flew to her brother.

As she drove to the airport on Fridays and rode to it with her father on Sundays, fear scattered her grief: it lay beside her, hovered behind her. Shards of it stayed in her body; she could touch the places they pierced in her brain and heart. But fear was in her blood, her muscles, her breath. She heard herself speak to airline clerks. She did not make up anything; she did not look at the eyes or the posture of other passengers to find the one whose number was up and visible, or the one who wanted to die by explosion in a crowded plane. She did not imagine the plane's sudden fall, her back to the stars, her face to the earth, the seat belt squeezing her double as she waited for words to utter before the earth she loved tore her apart. She only breathed, and moved onto the plane, always to an aisle seat.

The width and height of the aisle held breath and light, and she gazed at it. On her other side were shadow and two people filling two seats, a bulkhead with a dark glass window, an overhead whose curve sealed her. For two hours she flew to the city where her brother was dying. She drank wine and looked at the aisle.

Her brother was dying from love. At first she had watched her parents' eyes for shame, but she saw only the lights of grief. Mortality had raised him from his secrets; there was nothing to hide, and he lay whole between clean sheets. It was she who left parts of her behind when she entered the house. Her brother was two years older than she, and he was thin and weak in his bed. She did not see fear in his eyes anymore. For a long time it had been there, a wet brightness she wanted to consume with her body. He looked at her as though death were a face between them, staring back at him. Sitting on the bed, she bent through death and held her thin brother. Her breasts felt strong and vital, and she wanted to absorb his fear and give him life. She held him as if this were possible. She did not know when fear left him, but it had. Now wit and mischief were in his eyes again, and a new and brighter depth. She did not know what it was. She only knew it was good to see. Sometimes she believed it was simply that:

goodness itself, as though death were stripping him of all that was dark and base, mean and vain, not only in him but in the world, too, in its parts that touched his life.

So she felt she could tell him now: she was afraid to fly. She was holding his hand. He smiled at her. He said: "Fear is a ghost; embrace your fear, and all you'll see in your arms is yourself." They could have been sitting at her kitchen table, drinking wine. He could have been saying: *Read Tolstoy; lie in the sun; make love only with one you love.* He had told her that, drinking wine at her table, years ago. She looked at his face on the pillow, wanting to see him as he had seen himself, holding his fear in his arms. She saw her brother dying.

On the plane going home, she folded her arms beneath her breasts. Then she closed her eyes and hugged. She saw herself buckled into the seat, under the tight arc of the plane's body. She saw the plane in the immense sky, then her brother in bed, poised as she was between the gravity of earth and infinity. She had tried with a poem to know his fear, months ago, when she could still write. But the poem changed, became one about love, and the only fear in it was hers, of loving again, of her heart swelling to be pierced and emptied.

Lightly embracing herself, she saw that, too: the words of the poem coming from her pen, the notebook and her forearms and hands resting on the oak desk her grandmother had used, writing letters. She saw her grandmother, long dead now, writing with a fountain pen. She saw herself sitting in the classroom, at the desk where some afternoons chalk dust lay, and she brushed it off with notepaper so it would not mark the sleeves of her sweater. A trace of someone who had taught before her, who nervously handled chalk. Traces of herself were scattered in the world. She saw the book she had published, held open by hands she would never know. She saw herself holding her last lover, under blankets on a cold night, waking with him to start a day.

She liked starting: a poem, a class, a meal for friends who crowded her kitchen while she cooked. But not starting a day, now that she was alone. She woke from night and dreams to the beginning of nothing. For minutes she lay in bed, gathering her scattered self. Then she rose to work, to be with friends. She liked the touch of leather boots on her calves, soft wool on her arms, snow on her face.

She wondered what her brother saw, now that fear had left his eyes. Her grandmother's eyes were like his, when she was old but not visibly dying: She seemed to watch from a mirthful distance. Perhaps connected to wherever she was going, she still took pleasure in the sport of mortality. Maybe it was a gift, for those who had lived long, and those who were slowly dying. She wanted it while her body was strong, while she was vibrant and pretty. Hugging herself, her eyes closed, she wanted it now as she breathed in this shuddering plane, speeding through darkness under the stars. She was afraid until the plane stopped on the runway.

The Colonel's Wife

FOR NICOLE

THE RETIRED MARINE COLONEL HAD TWO broken legs, both in casts from the soles of his feet to the tops of his thighs. His name was Robert Townsend; he was a tall and broad-shouldered man with black hair and a graying mustache. In the hospital in Boston he had five operations; neither leg was healed enough to bear his weight; he had rods in both femurs and his right tibia, and now at home he was downstairs in the living room on a hospital bed whose ends he could raise and lower, to evade pain. The bed was narrow, and his golden-haired wife, Lydia, slept upstairs.

He refused to eat in bed, for this made him feel he was still in the hospital; so at mealtimes Lydia helped him onto the wheelchair. He raised the bed till he was upright, she handed him a short board with beveled

ends, and he pushed one end under his rump and
rested the other on the chair. Then she held his legs
while he worked himself across the board. He wore cotton gym shorts and T-shirts. Before the horse fell on
him, he and Lydia had eaten breakfast and lunch at the
kitchen table. He could not go there now. He could
wheel through the door from the dining room to the
kitchen; then his long legs, held by leg rests straight out
in front of him, were blocked by a counter, and at his
left the refrigerator stopped him. On his first morning
at home he tried to turn between the counter and refrigerator by lowering the leg rests; when he pressed the
switch to release them, they dropped quickly, and he
gasped at the blades of pain in his falling legs. Lydia
bent down and grabbed his ankles and lifted them
while he moaned and began to sweat.

His feet in their casts would not fit under the long
rectangular mahogany table in the dining room, so he
sat parallel to his end of it, removed the right armrest
of the wheelchair, and ate, as he said, sidesaddle. He
looked to his right at his food and Lydia. She had
brown eyes and had lately, in the evening, worn her
hair in a French braid; she liked candles at dinner, and
after her bath in late afternoon she wore a dress or skirt.
Her face was tan and pink, her brow and cheek
creased, and lines moved outward from her eyes and
lips when she smiled. Every morning after breakfast she
walked two miles east to a red country store. She did
this in all weather except blizzards and lightning
storms. At the store she bought the *New York Times* and
a package of British cigarettes, and sat at the counter
to drink coffee and read. Then she walked home for
lunch, and came in the front door each day as precisely

as a clock striking noon. She had not done this since the sunlit morning of January thaw when Robert's brown mare broke his legs.

To Robert's left, while he ate, was the living room, and to his rear the kitchen. Behind Lydia was a large window, and the wide and deep back lawn ending at woods. They had four acres with many trees and they could not see their neighbors' houses; even now, in winter, there were enough evergreens so all the earth they saw from the house was their own. Before dinner Lydia drew the curtains at her back; she felt exposed through the glass. On Robert's second night at home, he asked her to open the curtains; he said he was sorry, but the covered window reminded him of the hospital. The hospital had been very difficult. He had served in two wars without being injured, and had never been confined to a hospital. Now when he saw the curtains behind Lydia, he felt enclosed by something that would take away his breath.

He could wheel slowly down the carpeted hall that began where the living and dining rooms joined, but the hall was too narrow for him to turn into the rooms it led to; one of these was a bathroom. He longed for a shower, and never felt truly clean. He kept a plastic urinal hooked by its handle over a railing of the bed, and Lydia emptied and cleaned it. For most of his four weeks and five days in the hospital, he had to use a bedpan, and nurses cleaned him. In his last week, the physical therapist and a nurse helped him from his wheelchair onto a hospital commode; they removed the inside arms from the chair and the commode, pushed the transfer board under him, and held his legs as he moved across. Then they propped his legs on pillows on a chair and left him alone. He had to use both hands to push himself up from the seat, so when the two women returned, they held his legs and tilted him and the nurse wiped him. Now he did this in the living room with Lydia. He knew Lydia did not mind wiping him, she was cheerful and told him to stop feeling humiliated because his legs were broken and he had to shit. But his stench and filth, and the intimacy of her hands and voice, slapped his soul with a wet cloth.

Five mornings a week, a home health aid woman helped him wash and shave on the bed. The housekeeper came on three mornings, and worked upstairs while the woman bathed him. A visiting nurse took his blood pressure and temperature and pulse. A phone was on the bedside table, and his son and two daughters called him often; they had flown to Boston to see him during his first week in the hospital. On some nights friends came; they tired him, but he needed these men and women. He felt removed from the earth as he had known it, and they brought parts of it with them: its smell was on their coats and hats and scarves, its color in their cheeks, its motion in their beautiful and miraculous legs.

During his first ten days at home, Lydia left the house only to buy groceries, and she did that while someone was with him. Then on a Friday night, while they were eating dinner, he said: "I'm starting to feel like a cage. I want you to walk to the store tomorrow."

"It's Saturday. You'd be alone."

"I've got the phone and a urinal."

"I don't want you to feel alone."

"I'll be fine."

Next morning she hung a second urinal on the bed

railing, put a pitcher of water and a pitcher of orange juice and two glasses on the bedside table, and wrote the phone number of the store on notepaper. She was wearing jeans and boots and a dark blue sweater. She bent over him and looked at his eyes.

"Listen: if you have to shit, you call me. I'll be through the door in twenty-eight minutes."

She kissed him and put on a blue parka and black beret, and he watched over his right shoulder as she went out the door. He lay facing the mahogany table and the dining room window and the winter light. He could not see the lawn, but he could see trunks and branches of deciduous trees and the green pines. His wheelchair was beside the bed, the transfer board resting on it, but he could not go to the stove, could not even get far enough into the kitchen to see it, and for breakfast they ate scrambled eggs; Lydia always turned off burners and the oven, but in his career he had learned to check everything, even when he knew it was done. He had not thought of fire till Lydia was gone, and Lydia had not thought of fire, and he saw himself in the wheelchair pushing away from flames. The back door was in the kitchen, so he could leave only through the front; outside was a deck and four steps to the concrete walk that curved to the long driveway. He closed his eyes and breathed deeply into his stomach and told himself: *Proper planning prevents piss-poor performance.* Years ago in California, a gunnery sergeant had said that to the company at morning formation; Robert was a second lieutenant, watching from the barracks porch; the gunny had fought in the Pacific, and Robert, unblooded still, looked at the man's broad, straight back and believed this was a message brought from the dread and chaos of war. *I can call the fire department, then get on the wheelchair, take the blanket, go out the front door, and sit on the deck and wait for the firemen; if it gets bad, I'll tuck my chin and go bass-ackwards down the steps and hope the casts hold and I don't crack my head; then if I have to, I can drag myself all the way to the fucking road.* He opened his eyes and looked around the room. He was still afraid, and for a while he read *War and Peace.* Then he slept, and he was dreaming of white-trousered soldiers on horses when Lydia opened the door. He was happy to see her, and he said nothing about fire. He said nothing about it when she walked to the store Sunday morning; and when she went Monday, the home health aid woman and housekeeper were with him for all but the last hour.

He had started reading *War and Peace* a week before his horse slipped and fell on his left leg, scrambled upright, then slipped again and fell on both his legs; then Robert was screaming, and finally the horse got up and watched him. Then he moaned, and breathed in quick rhythm with the pain, and called toward the stables beyond a stand of trees, called "Help," and knew he had screamed under the horse because he could not move, and such helplessness felt like drowning in sunlit air near the shadows of pines. In the hospital he had morphine and now, in the bedside table Lydia had carried downstairs, he had Demerol and Percodan. When pain cut through his concentration so he could not focus on talking with Lydia, he took Percodan; when pain was all he could feel of his body, and it filled his brain and spirit so he moaned and tried not to yell, he took Demerol. Always there was pain in his legs, but if he kept them elevated and did not move his body, it was bearable for hours at a time, and he read; and, resting from that, he looked out the dining room window, and at the mahogany table.

He had never had any feelings about the things of domestic life. In them he saw Lydia's choices, and his admiration was not for the objects but for her. If all the furniture in the house were carried off by thieves, his only sorrow would be for Lydia. She had bought the mahogany table early in their marriage. She had money, and when each grandparent and parent died, she accumulated more. The table had traveled in moving vans back and forth across the nation. It had remained unmarked by children, and by officers and their wives from Hawaii to Virginia; it had stood amid family quarrels and silence and laughter, amid boisterous drinking and storytelling and flirtations, and here it was, in this house in the country north of Boston, without a scar. He had lived with it for decades, and now, lying helpless and in pain, he began to feel affection for the table. In the morning he opened his eyes to it; at night in the dark he looked at its shape in the pale light of the window as he waited for one drug to release him from pain and another to give him sleep.

The shock of the horse crushing his bones, then anesthesia, surgery, pain, and drugs had taken his vitality. He could not finish a meal, he could not remain either awake or alert from morning till night, he did not want to smoke a pipe or drink a martini, and he could not feel passion for Lydia. One night in his third week at home, when she bent to kiss him good night, he held her to his chest, his cheek pressing hers, and all his feeling for her was above his loins, filling his breast, and one or two joyful tears moistened his eyes. Then he watched her cross the room to the stairs; she wore dark shades of brown: a sweater and skirt and tights and high-heeled boots. He watched her climb to the hall and disappear into the light she turned on at the top of the stairs. He listened to her footsteps going to the bedroom; then the hall was dark again, and his bedside lamp was the only light in the house; it warmed his cheek.

He had not climbed the stairs for two months, and now he saw that all of the second floor was Lydia's: the bedroom, the large bathroom with its sweet scents of things for her body, her room where she read and wrote letters and paid bills. Always she had paid the bills, and this had nothing to do with her inheritance; it was common for officers' wives to manage all elements of the household, so the man could be rushed off to war without pausing to brief his wife on debts, automobile maintenance, and so on. Upstairs were a sunporch, a television room with a wet bar, and two guest bedrooms. For three years he had inhabited that floor. But Lydia had given of herself to those spaces enclosed by wood and glass, colored by paint and light, and he felt they were mysteriously alive and female.

Then he realized this was true of the first floor as well. At cocktail hour he had mixed drinks in the kitchen, and sometimes cooked there or on the patio with charcoal; but certainly the kitchen was hers. So were the dining and living rooms and, down the hall, the bedroom and study and the bathroom, where he had showered after fishing or hunting or riding, lifting weights or running. Only his den, at the end of the hall, was truly his: the pipe stands and humidor on the desk, the ashtray always emptied, the desktop clear; the rifles and shotguns, pistols and revolvers locked behind wood and glass; the barbell and weights and bench; the closet door closed and behind it tackle boxes and boots, waders and running shoes on the floor, and, on hangers above them, the clothing of his passions. His fishing rods hung on pegs on one wall, his hats and caps on pegs on another, above a bookcase filled with literature of war. His rear wall was glass and through it he could see nearly all of the back lawn and watch squirrels on trees in the woods, crows, gliding hawks; sometimes a doe suddenly appeared at the edge of the woods and Robert Townsend watched it with joy.

Every other room in the house was female. If he closed his den, removed his things from the downstairs bathroom, and lowered the toilet seat, there would be no sign of a man in the house. In the warmth of the bedside lamp, he smiled: probably he never would have made this discovery if he had not lost the freedom of walking in his home. They could not have built the house without her money; but her money had never been important to him; it had come with her, like her golden hair, and if she lost it, he would love her as dearly as he would when her hair yellowed and grayed and no longer shone in the sun. The money had spared him worry about the children's education, and the nuisance of worn-out cars and appliances; but it did not touch what he loved in his life; his salary was sufficient for that. Reading *War and Peace* drew from him a comparison between himself and Lydia, and Tolstoy's officers and ladies; Lydia's money had given them the ease, the grace, of the aristocracy. But it had not spared them the rigors and the uprootings of military life, the sorrow of two wars, and the grief for dead friends and their widows and children, and for the men he had lost: men who were like sons he was given when they were eighteen, boys whom he loved for only months before they died. Their names and faces stayed in his heart; if you looked closely at his eyes, you could see them. Lydia knew his grief well, and tenderly; were it not part of him, she may have loved him less.

He took a sleeping pill and turned off the bedside lamp. He liked this new way of seeing the house, as if the entire structure were female and he entered it to be at its center with Lydia; and she had made a place for him, his den, as she gave him a place in her body. A great tenderness welled in him. He regretted his rebukes of Lydia, through the years, and his infidelities when he was alone overseas. These were with prostitutes. He had acted in privacy and had never told anyone. Afterward, he had forgiven himself in the same way that, on hungover mornings, he had absolved himself for being a drunken fool: he sloughed off remorse as he shaved his whiskers; then he put on his uniform and went to work. He did not justify his adultery; he believed a better man would have been chaste; but he saw it as an occupational hazard of soldiering. He was an active man, and his need for a woman's love was nocturnal, or it seemed to be. But during months of separation from Lydia, that need moved into daylight: a tender loneliness, a sense of being unattached, of floating near the boundaries of fear. Also, Robert Townsend loved women: a woman's eyes could move his blood as the moon pulls the sea. It was neither easy nor simple for him to live for a year without the nakedness of a woman; he had done his best, and on more than a thousand nights he had prevailed.

He wished this night, drugged in the living room, that he had been perfect, that he had made love with no one since he met Lydia on a blind date in La Jolla. He was a second lieutenant wearing dress blues, the date was for the Marine Corps birthday ball, and while his friend waited in the car, he strode up the long walk to the lighted front door; she was living with her parents still, and he was unabashed by the size of the stone house, its expanse of lawn and accumulation of trees. In his left hand, he held his white gloves and her corsage. He rang the doorbell, then stepped back so she would see the height and breadth of him when she swung open the door. Behind him was the ocean, and he smelled it with every breath. Then she opened the door: she was in a silver gown with a full skirt, he was smelling her perfume, and he looked at her tanned face and arms and golden hair and felt that he was looking at the sun without burning his eyes.

In the hospital the surgeon told Robert that his knees would not fully recover, his left one would probably never bend more than forty degrees, and he would live more comfortably in a one-story home. The surgeon was a trim young man with gentle brown eyes; Robert liked him, and told him not to worry about an old Marine climbing a flight of stairs. One afternoon when Lydia was in the room, the surgeon talked about stairs and Robert's knees again, looking at her. He said there would also be atrophy of the legs because the casts would not come off for months. Then, until Robert came home, Lydia looked at houses and land, but she did not love any of it. She spoke to the building contractor, and phoned orthopedic surgeons in Arizona, near her family ranch.

Now she talked of their going to the ranch and staying there while the contractor removed the second floor and put those rooms on the ground. Robert believed his knees would be as they had always been until they were broken, and while Lydia talked about Arizona, he was eating without hunger but to gain strength, or pushing a urinal between the casts on his thighs, or feeling pain from his feet to his crotch. Every day and night he thought of men he had seen wounded in war. He had never told Lydia about them, and he did not tell her now. How many times had he yelled for corpsmen, and controlled his horror, and done everything he could to help, and everything correctly? He knew now that his horror had kept him separate from the torn meat and broken bones that an instant ago were a man, strong and quick; and kept him, too, from telling Lydia. Now his own pain opened him up, and pity flowed from him, washed timeless over those broken men lying on the earth.

On a Saturday morning in his fifth week at home, while they were eating breakfast, snow began to fall. When Lydia walked to the store, he watched the snow through the dining room window, then slept. He woke to the sound of Lydia's boots on the front steps. He looked to his right and behind him at the door as she opened it: she was looking down at her gloved hand on the knob, snow was quickly melting on her shoulders and beret and hair, her cheeks were flushed, and her brightened eyes were seeing something that was not in the room, some image or memory, and fear rose from his stomach, he felt shackled to the bed, and suddenly he was sweating. Then she looked at him, and came quickly to him, took his hand, and said: "What is it?"

"My legs."

"Did you take something?"

"No."

Her brown shoulder bag was damp, bulging at her side; always he had teased her about crammed purses; now this one seemed filled with secrets that could destroy him. She placed a palm on his brow.

"It's passing," he said. "It'll be all right."

"Are you hungry?"

"No."

"Try something."

"I will."

She smelled of snow and winter air. She unzipped her parka and climbed the stairs. He shut his eyes and saw nothing; but nameless fear rushed in his blood. He listened to Lydia's footsteps going to the bathroom. She was wearing her moccasins. She flushed the toilet, washed her hands, and he watched the head of the stairs, focused on the spot where her face would appear; then it was there, descending, and in her eyes and mouth he saw nothing. He had been in bed for too long—this fear must be madness—and when she helped him onto the chair, he looked away from her, at the dining room window, the falling snow.

He watched it while she was in the kitchen. She brought black bean soup she had made the night before, and a green salad and hot rolls. He dipped a spoon into the soup and raised it to his mouth and swallowed; he put the spoon down and ate a piece of roll, then a slice of cucumber. He kept doing this, his head turned to watch her smile and talk and chew, until he had eaten everything. Then she helped him onto the bed, and cleared the table; he listened to her putting the dishes in the dishwasher. He closed his eyes before she came into the living room; he felt her looking at him as she walked to the stairs; then she climbed them and went down the hall to her room. He did not want to be awake, and soon he slept. When he woke, snow was still falling; it was gathering wetly on the pine branches; the house was quiet and as dark as it could be in midafternoon with so many windows. He turned on the lamp. Pain squeezed his bones, and his heart was breaking. Lydia's face when she opened the door at noon was the face that for years he had given her: that blush of her cheeks, and light in her eyes. He knew she had a lover.

He listened to the house. She was in it, but where was she? She could be in her room, the door closed, talking on the phone to—He could not imagine a man. He wanted to feel rage and jealousy, but all he felt was absolute helplessness and dread and sorrow. He held the phone and slowly lifted the receiver and listened to the dial tone as he stared at the snow. He opened the table's top drawer, got the bottle of Percodan, and shook one into his palm. He saw himself as he would look to Lydia: a man in pain, lying on his back with casts on his legs, reaching for the glass of water beside him; a man whose stinking shit she cleaned from the commode and wiped from his body. For nearly three hours the images had waited, perched and watching just beyond his ken, and now they gathered and assaulted him, and he breathed deeply and fast, and opened and closed his hands, and saw in the snow and the pines Lydia making love.

The hall upstairs was darkened; the only sound in the house was his breath. All his life with her he had believed he knew where she was. When he was at a desk eight miles away from her or drinking coffee from a canteen cup at dawn in Vietnam, he imagined her in their home, or within its natural boundaries. She was at a wives' luncheon or tea, or in a restaurant for lunch with one or two women; she was walking—she had always loved a long walk alone and, since their courtship, had walked more miles than Robert, an infantryman, and this was a family joke; she was sitting with a cup of tea before the fire, or iced tea on the lawn; she was buying dresses, blouses, sweaters, bracelets, necklaces with the endearing pleasure he saw in his daughters, too, before they could spell what they wore; she was making peanut butter sandwiches for the children home from school; she was talking on the phone held between her shoulder and ear while she sautéed onions. In his three years of retirement, his view of her had not changed; he did not know that till now. He had been hunting and fishing with new friends, had bought the mare and boarded her, read books, written letters to friends, and waked some mornings feeling surprised, disoriented, and tardy. He had worked each day with his body and mind, and at sunset had turned to Lydia's merry brown eyes and the mingled scents from her bath. He knew her face when she slept; when she woke in the morning; when she was pale and sick; when fatigue hung like weights from her eyes and cheeks. Yet when he handed her a martini and looked at her red

lips and shaded eyelids, and smelled her, he did not
think of bottles and tubes and boxes on her dressing
table. This face, these smells, were her at sunset. He
called into the darkness, his voice soft and high, crest-
ing on his fear: "Lydia?"

He could not bear the pain in his legs, not with this,
and he called her name again and again and again,
and the nothing he heard was so quiet, and he listened
so intently to it, he believed he could hear the snow
falling. It would fall until it covered the house, until the
power lines broke from their poles, and he would die
here, not from cold or hunger or thirst, but because he
was alone and could not move. Then he was sobbing
into his hands, and he heard only that and so was star-
tled as by an angel of death when Lydia's hands
gripped his wrists and strongly and gently pulled his
hands from his eyes; then her voice was in his heart:
"Bob," she said. "Bobby."

He held her. He pulled himself upward and groaned
as the pain tightened and turned in his broken bones,
he pressed his face to her breasts, and Lydia's arms
came around him. Her hands moved up and down his
back. He heard her tears when she said: "I fell asleep.
I didn't hear you. I'm sorry. I'm so sorry this happened
to you. I'm so sorry about your *knees*."

Grief shook her body in his arms. He wanted to
stand and hold her face at his chest, stroke her hair,
speak softly to her. He sniffed tears and swallowed
them, moved his head from her breast, looked up at
her wet cheeks and eyes and trembling mouth, and he
lowered his arms and with a hand patted the sheet beside him.

"Here," he said. "Here. Lie down."

She lay beside him, and the first touch of her weight on the bed moved his legs, and he clenched his teeth and swallowed a groan and kept silent. Her head lay on his right bicep, and he brought that hand to her face and hair. His fingers lightly rubbed her tears. He closed his eyes and in that darkness saw snow, and felt his legs; but above them he was emptied of pain, and now he did not see snow or darkness, but sunlight in La Jolla, and Lydia as a small golden-haired child on that vast and shaded lawn; then he saw her gray and thin and dying in pain. In the orthopedic ward people screamed, and many nights he had pushed the call button again and again and finally cried out for a nurse to give him morphine. He did not know whether or not there were atheists in foxholes; he believed now there must have been many in field hospitals, and in the naval hospitals afterward, and in the hospital he had come home from so long ago. In Korea and Vietnam, it was Lydia he prayed to, if turning in fear and loneliness to someone was prayer. Certainly it was hope and faith and love. He felt these now, with his eyes closed, holding Lydia, seeing her weeping above his bed, her body slowly falling toward him as he patted the sheet; seeing the lines of her face she said were from smoking and the sun, but they were time, too. She loved him; and if he had never known precisely where she was, she had finally always been here. Then her head and body jerked and she was keening, and he opened his eyes to immense sound, and the lamplight, the darkness in the dining room, the snow: "You won't be able to climb those fucking stairs. *You* can. But it'll be awful, it's awful, it's awful, you don't know how badly you're *hurt*, Bob, you don't know, because it's you, it's you—"

She stopped. He waited until she was no longer crying and her breath was slow again, then said softly: "I know about you."

"You do?"

"I know you're having an affair."

"That's all it is. It just ended."

"Because my legs are broken?"

"I don't know. Yes. Because your legs are broken." She held her breath for a moment, then released it. "It's not my first."

"No."

"I need a cigarette for this."

His body started to sit up, to rise from the bed and climb the stairs to get her purse. Then she was gone, to her room, then the bathroom, and she came down with fresh makeup and her cigarettes, and lay beside him and looked at his eyes. She said: "I've never loved anyone else."

"I've cheated, too."

"I know."

"What do you know?"

"Japan. Okinawa. Hong Kong. Vietnam. Maybe some in the States."

"Not in the States. How did you know?"

"I'm your wife."

"Why didn't I know?"

"Because I'm your wife. How much do you want to hear?"

"I want to hear everything, and go to Arizona, and sleep in the same bed with you."

Now his heartbreak was like the pain in his legs: it was part of him, but he could breathe with it, think with it, listen and see with it. Until the light outside faded, and darkness gathered around the lamp at the bed, her voice rose softly from the pillow, and snow moved outside the window. When she told him she had never had a lover while he was at war, Robert said: "In case I got killed?"

"Yes. I just didn't know I had to include riding a horse," and laughter came to them as suddenly as weeping had. It took their breath, it drew tears from them, it shook his body and hurt his bones, and he held Lydia and laughed.

A week later, they were in Arizona, watching purple spread over a mountain range in the sunset. They were on the patio; she lit coals on the grill and stepped back from the flames, then poured martinis from the pitcher and sat beside him. He looked at the mountain and sun and sky, then looked at her eyes and told her of maimed and dying boys, of holding them while their lives flowed out of them, onto snow, grass, mud. He told her of terror that came like thunder after lightning, after the explosions and gunfire, after everything was done. He told her of his terror under the horse, and on the bed in their living room when he was alone in the house. He said: "I'm glad that damned horse fell on me. It made me lie still in one place and look at you."

"I hope you haven't seen too much."

"There's never too much. There's not enough time."

"No."

"Time makes us the same, you and me. That's all I know."

He knew this: sunlight on the twist of lemon in her glass as she lifted it by the stem and brought it to her red lips. On the day the snow fell till midnight, she had made no promises, and had not asked any of him. He did not want promises. They were words and feelings wafting about in a season he or Lydia may not live to see. He wanted only to know what had happened and what was happening now, to see that: brilliant as the sky, hot as the sun, bright as Lydia's eyes.

The Lover

LEE TRAMBATH WAS A FIFTY-FIVE-YEAR-OLD restaurant manager, with three ex-wives and five children. He was a slender, dark-haired man with a trimmed beard that was mostly gray, and he lived and worked in a small Massachusetts town, near the sea. The children were from his first two marriages, three daughters and two sons, grown now and spread up and down the eastern seaboard from Charleston to Portland, all in places he liked to visit. None of them was married; they all had lovers. Lee was on good terms with the two mothers of his children; time had healed him, had allowed him to forget whatever he and the women had done to each other, or removed the precision of pain from his memory; and sometimes, sitting alone in his apartment or strolling on the boardwalk along the river flowing a mile or so to the ocean, he wished as a boy does: that in some way his first marriage had never ended, yet his second had occurred so the daughter and son from that one would be on the earth; and that he and the two women and five children were one family. This frequent wish was never erotic: his images were of him and the two women and five children in living rooms, dining rooms, on lawns. It was the third wife, and the women in their forties whom he dated after his divorce from her, who made him refer to his last marriage as absolutely his last.

His third wife was nearly forty when they married; she had two daughters who were aging her with their listless work in high school, slovenly lives at home, strong-willed disobedience, and unsavory boyfriends, whose tight clothing seemed only a cover to get from their cars to the house and, with the girls, back to their cars. Lee did what he could, with tender hesitance; the girls' father had moved to Houston when they were six and eight, and sent them checks on birthdays and at Christmas. Lee silently predicted pregnancies, abortions, and a few years of too much drinking and cocaine. Then after college, which even they would be able to attend and muddle through, they would work at jobs to pay for clothes, cars, and apartments; and, like most people, they would settle softly into mundane lives. For Lee, the household was often frenzied and barely tolerable, with three females crying at once, but he was forty-nine, he had spent most of his adult life with families, and he could bear it.

His wife did not hold up as well, and told him to get a vasectomy. He did not want to. Gently and reasonably he said he would not mind being sterile if it simply happened to him, if nature retired him from the ranks of fertility; but he did not want it done to him by a doctor; and, more importantly, he did not want to choose to have it done, but this was a hair he could not split for her. She was not gentle, and if her argument was reasonable, her scorn for his feelings, her crying and cursing him for not loving her, made reason hard to discern. She would not make love with him until he gave in; and he did, because he understood her fears more than he understood his resistance, and he wanted to keep peace, so when he consented, he began to see her demand as a request that could not be made calmly. Who could turn away from a drowning woman because her plea for help came not as a whisper but a scream? Undressing for surgery, he felt he was giving up his life as he had known it; and afterward, when he brought his sperm to be tested, he hoped the surgeon had failed; or, rather, that his sperm remained, undaunted by scalpel, or his wife, or himself. His wife was relieved, and soon he was, too, and peace returned, or they returned to it.

When it did not last, when its not lasting slowly burned to ashes all kindness and respect in the marriage, when the marriage ended and Lee Trambath was in a bachelor apartment again, and seeing his two stepdaughters there and in restaurants, and dating again, he thought of his vasectomy as a concealed deformity, something he was hiding from women. No one he dated wanted more children, but still he always felt he was dissembling, until he told them, and one and all looked into his eyes as though he had spread yellow roses between them on the bar, the dinner table, or the bed.

He had married his first two wives when they were in their twenties, and he was the first husband of both; and always, however small, the shadows of sadness and failure were cast upon him: all his love and serious intent had increased the population of divorcées by two. His union with his third wife was his first with a divorcée; and her ex-husband, or what he had done to her, or what she believed he had done to her with no provocation at all, was a fulcrum in her marriage to Lee: he could trace the extremities of her anger and sorrow to that man he had never known. Now, dating, he collided with the presence of a man, or men, he only knew because a woman was pouting or crying or yelling or throwing a kitchen utensil at him, once a pot holder, once a breadboard. The pain and bitterness, fear and distrust, of these women seemed all to be caused by one of his gender, not only husbands and lovers, but fathers and stepfathers as well. Confronted by these lives in which not one woman, including the woman herself, had ever been anything but kind, generous, and consoling, he began not only to believe it but to feel responsible for it, and he tried to atone. No one he dated ever accused him of being harsh, cruel, inattentive. They praised his patient listening, his lack of fear and cynicism in the face of love. They never accused him of anything; still they made him feel like a drugged coral snake, sleeping and beautiful, which they took the risk of wearing around their throats while the clock ticked and the effect of the drug subsided: with the first slow movement of his flesh, they would grab him and hold him on the table and, with an oyster fork, pierce his brain.

He began to wonder what he had done to his wives.

The first had never remarried, had kept his last name, and for the past seventeen years had lived on Cape Cod with one man. The second had married again, and the third was dating. What cracks had he left in their hearts? Did they love less now and settle for less in return, as they held on to parts of themselves they did not want to give and lose again? Or—and he wished this—did they love more fully because they had survived pain, so no longer feared it? This could not be true of his third wife: she would need a strong, gentle, and older man, someone like a father without the curse of incest. But perhaps the first two wives were free of him, were saved. Lee was so afraid of what he might have done to his daughters, even his stepdaughters, whose lives he had entered when they were already in motion at a high and directionless speed, that he wondered about them as he did about the time and manner of his death: seldom, and with either terrible images or a silent blankness in his mind, like a window covered with shining white paint. With the women he loved after his last marriage, he started smoking again, and drinking more.

There were three of these women, separated by short intervals of pain, remorse, and despair. When he and the last one had their final quarrel—she threw the breadboard—he was nearly fifty-five, and he gave up on love, save the memory of it. Always his aim had been marriage. He had never entered what he considered to be an affair, something whose end was an understood condition of its beginning. But he had loved and wanted for the rest of his life women who took him in their arms, and even their hearts, but did not plan to keep him. He had known that about them, they had told him no lies about what they wanted, and he had persisted, keeping his faith: if he could not change their hearts, then love itself would.

As a young man, in his first marriage, he had done some erotic dabbling: one-night stands whose causes, he now knew, were alcohol, night, and vanity. This had only scratched his marriage: a little blood showed, nothing more; for his wife had also fallen from grace, and in the same way. Theirs was a confessional marriage, and the purging of one and forgiving by the other deepened their love. The marriage ended much later, when their sexual mischief was far behind them, and Lee would never understand all of its ending any more than he could explain why, on their first date in college, there was already enough love between them to engender the years it would take to have three children and let their love die. He learned how quickly love died when you weren't looking; if you weren't looking.

At the restaurant a flaxen-haired young waitress flirted with him as a matter of course. This was Doreen Brodie. She was tall, and her limbs looked stronger than his. Some nights he had an after-hours drink with her, sitting at the bar, and her blue eyes and thin red lips aroused his passion and, more tempting, swelled his loneliness till it nearly brimmed over, nearly moved his arms to hold her. He did not touch her. She was younger than his children; he was old, a marital leftover wearing a jacket and tie.

He had come to believe that only young women still trusted love, believed in it. He knew this could not be true, that it was the inductive reasoning of his bad luck, that he simply had not met resilient older women because they lived someplace else, or lived here in this little town but somehow had not crossed his path. Yet even if he met such a woman, wasn't he the common denominator in three divorces? Perhaps he was a sleeping snake. He slipped into masturbation and nearly always, afterward, felt he was too old for this, too, and what he wiped from his hand onto the sheet was his dignity. But sometimes on long afternoons when he could think of nothing but Doreen Brodie, of phoning her and asking her for a date, of having dinner with her, of making love with her, and so falling in love with her, he resorted to the dry and heartless caress of his hand; then, his member spent and limp as his soul, he focused clearly on his life again, and he did not call Doreen.

He had married friends and went to their homes for dinner, or joined them at bars, but mostly he was alone in his apartment. So working nights, which had been an intrusion on his marriages and an interference with his dating, became a blessing. He started reading history or philosophy during the day, going for long walks, and keeping a journal in spiral notebooks. He wrote every morning before breakfast: reflections on what he read, on people at the restaurant, sketches of the town and river and sky as he saw them on his walks. He wrote slowly, used a large dictionary, and took pleasure in precise nouns, verbs, and adjectives. He liked working with colors. He wrote nothing painful or erotic; he did not want his children to feel pity or shame when they went through his effects after his death. For a summer and fall, a winter and part of a spring, Lee Trambath lived like this, till an April morning when he woke to the sound and smell of rain.

As he dressed he remembered that yesterday he had

meant to buy coffee, but, drawn by sunshine and a salty breeze from the sea, he had walked along the river, instead of to the store. He wanted to write about rain, try to put its smell and sound on paper. But he had no coffee, and he put on his raincoat and a felt hat and went downstairs and outside. At once his face and throat and hands were pleasantly wet. Across the street was the gray river. He watched rain falling on it, and cars moving slowly, their headlights glowing. Then he walked to the end of the block and turned left, onto the main street. He smelled rain and the sea. The grocery store was in the next block, but his stride was slowing as he approached a newsstand with a kitchen for breakfast and lunch. In front of it, he stopped. Until nearly a year ago he had come here for breakfast, read newspapers, bought paperback books. Some time after he ducked the breadboard and backed out of her kitchen, backed out of her dining and living rooms and front door, he had begun his rituals of abstinence: his journal; his breakfast at home; his study of America, hoping to find in that huge canvas perhaps one brush stroke to illuminate the mystery of his life; his walks, whose purpose was for at least one hour of light to see where he lived, smell it, touch it, listen to its sounds. Standing in the cool rain, he lost his eagerness to write about it, but he kept its thrill. The rain on his face was like joyful tears, given him by the clouds; he could not recall when he had last wept. Now a new excitement welled in him—that of a holiday—and he moved to the door and swung it open and went inside, looking first to his left at the counter for tobacco and boxed candy at that wall, and beyond it the shelves of magazines and racks of books; then he looked to his right at tables for two and four where people were eating, and a long counter facing a mirror. Seated at the counter were a policeman, a young couple looking at each other as they talked, a gray-haired man alone, and Doreen Brodie reading a newspaper. To her right were three empty stools. He walked between tables and sat beside her. He had never seen her in daylight, had never seen her anywhere save at the restaurant. She looked at the mirror opposite the counter, saw him there, smiled at his reflection, then turned the smile to him and said: "Well. What brings you out in the rain?"

He took off his hat and placed it on the counter and was about to say he was going to buy coffee, but he looked at Doreen's blue eyes and said: "I woke to the sound of rain. It was the first thing I smelled." From behind her a young waitress approached and he signaled with thumb and forefinger as if gripping a cup. "Some was splashing through the screen, onto the windowsill. I didn't close the window. I wanted to write about rain, but I was out of coffee." He was unbuttoning his coat, removing his arms from its sleeves. "I've been writing things. I wanted to write its smell and sound. Its feel in April." He let his coat fall to the back of his stool. The waitress brought his coffee, and he stopped talking to pay. She was a young brunette wearing glasses, probably a year out of high school and waiting, happily enough, it seemed, for something to happen. He looked at Doreen's eyes: "It would be a separate section; the rain. Coming right after something I wrote yesterday about William James. He said that fear doesn't cause running away. Running away causes fear. So if you hold your ground, you'll be brave. And that sadness doesn't cause crying. Crying makes us sad. So we should act the way we want to feel. And he said if that doesn't work, nothing else will anyway." Then he blushed. "He was a philosopher. I've been reading all kinds of things."

"Does it work?"

"What?"

"Acting the way you want to feel."

"Sometimes." He looked away from her, stirred sugar and cream into his cup. Still he felt her eyes.

"What is it you want to feel?"

Beneath his heart, wings fluttered. He looked at her eyes and the wings paused like a hawk's, and glided.

"You," he said, and they rushed in his breast, and someplace beneath them he felt the cool plume of a lie. "I want to feel you."

The lie spread upward, but light was in her eyes, and she was standing, was saying softly: "Let's go."

He stood and put on his coat and hat; she had a black umbrella; she left her newspaper on the counter and he followed her out the door. She opened the umbrella, held it between them, and he stepped under it. His arm touched hers; perhaps it was the first time he had ever touched her. He went with her up the street, away from the river; at the corner she stopped and faced traffic, and watched the red light. He looked at her profile. Suddenly he felt the solidity of the earth beneath his feet. Were gravity and grave rooted in the same word? In that moment, looking at her left eye and its long upturning lashes, her nose and lips, and the curve of her chin, he could have told her they must not do this, that he was a waste of her time, her fertility. Then she turned to him, and her eyes amazed him; he was either lost or found, he could not know which, and he surrendered.

The traffic light changed and they crossed the street and she led him down a brick alley between brick shops, then across a courtyard. His life was repeating itself, yet it felt not repetitious but splendid, and filled with grace. He lowered his eyes to rain moving on darkened bricks. *God in heaven,* he thought, *if there is one, bless us.* As a boy he was an Episcopalian. Then, with his first wife, he became his flesh and what it earned. Only his love for his children felt more spiritual than carnal. Holding one in his arms, he felt connected with something ancient, even immortal. In the arms of his passionate wife he felt a communion he believed was the supreme earthly joy. It had ended and he had found it again with other wives and other women, and always its ending had flung him into a dark pit of finitude, whose walls seeped despair as palpable as the rain he walked in now, after too many years.

Doreen's kiss dispelled those years. She gave it to him just across the threshold of her apartment, and he marveled at the resilience of nature. So many kisses in his lifetime, yet here he was, as though kissed for the first time on a front porch in summer in Dayton, Ohio. Oh plenitude, oh spring rain, and new love. He did not see the apartment: it was objects and shadows they moved through. Her unmade bed was box springs and a mattress on the floor, and quickly they were in it, his hat and clothes on the carpet with hers. He did not want it to end; he made love to her with his lips, his hands, his tongue. The muscles of her arms and stomach and legs were hard, her touch and voice soft; he spoke her name, he called her "sweet," he called her "my lovely," he perspired, and once from his stomach came a liquid moan of hunger. Finally she rolled away from him, toward the bedside table, and opened a drawer; he heard a tearing sound, and she sat up holding a golden condom.

"I have a vasectomy."

"What a guy. I've got an IUD."

"I've mostly been married."

"You never know." He watched her hands as she placed the condom and unrolled it. Then she kneeled above him, guided him in, and said: "I had given up on you."

"So had I."

Here it was again, the hot love of a woman, and he closed his eyes and saw the ocean at night, and squid mating on its gentle swell, a documentary he watched on television one afternoon last winter; sharks swam up and ate swaths of squid, but the others kept on, just kept on. *Fucking and eating,* he thought. They were why he left home, to marry and work, and here he was over thirty years later, with a woman nearly as young as his first wife when passion drove them out of their parents' homes and into the world, into a small apartment that was first an enclosure for their bed, and second for a kitchen to prepare food in and a table to eat it on, and third for plumbing so they could bathe, and flush body waste. All vitality radiated from the bed, enough of it to give him the drive and direction to earn money and father children; he fell in love with them, a love that was as much a component of his flesh as the flow of his blood; and in fact it could only end with that flow's ending. Now another flow was about to leave his body: the pleasure started in the muscles of his legs where masturbation never reached, and he saw the mockery of himself and his hand, and to rid his mind of this comparison he said her name. He said it again and again, naming her flesh and his delight, but the truth was as loud as their quick breath. His passion spurted from him, was gone, a bit of sterile liquid in a condom, a tiny bit if it were blood. It was enough to stain a sheet, make a child. His children would smile if they knew of this, if he told them he had waked to rain but had no coffee, so—There was nothing to smile about here. He opened his eyes. Doreen's were closed.

Soon he would soften inside her, and she was racing against the ebbing of his blood. He watched her face. Long ago he had learned that in lovemaking the one giving pleasure felt the greater intimacy; beyond a certain pitch of passion, the one receiving was isolated by muscles and nerves. He could have been watching her suffer pain; he could have been watching her die. She cried out. Then she was still, her eyes open, her breath deep and slowing. Before moving away, she reached between them and pinched the condom's opening. She took it with her, hanging from her fingers as she stood and smiled at him, and left the room.

He closed his eyes and listened to rain on the window. It saddened him now, all that rain and gray. He heard her footsteps in the hall, then soft on the carpet, and her lighter twice, and blown smoke; she sat on the bed and he spread his fingers for the cigarette; then she lay beside him and placed a cool glass ashtray on his stomach. He opened his eyes and looked at hers and said: "What more could I ask?"

"You could have asked sooner."

"I was trying to do something. Learn something. Do you know I could *own* a restaurant by now, if I wanted to? I never wanted to. I have money. I'm not just solvent; I have *money*. When I die, my children will be able to make down payments on houses. Big payments. I have five children. All grown, and none of them married. Nobody's in a hurry anymore. To marry."

"Nobody has to be."

"Exactly. And that's all I ever was. What are people now? Their jobs? I started behind the bar and in kitchens. Now I read all this stuff. History. Philosophy. Looking for myself, where I fit in. I must be part of it, right? I'm here. So I must be. You know where I fit? I earn and invest and spend money. You know why? Because I fell in love. When I was very young. If I hadn't, I might have joined the French Foreign Legion. Then I'd know, wouldn't I? What my part was. My part was this—" He gestured with a hand toward his penis; then he touched his heart. "And this. If you look at the country today, you see families torn apart. Kids with blood splashed on them. It all started with families. Like this, you and me, naked. People made love, settled land, built towns. Now the beginning is dying and we're left with the end. I'm part of that, too. Three divorces. So that's where I fit. At the beginning and the end. It was always love for me, love of a woman. I look back and I think love needs tenacity. Maybe that's what I didn't have. And where is love in all this? It's not here. You don't love me." Her eyes were gentle as she shook her head. "Probably I could love you. But what for? Reverse my vasectomy and start over? Own a restaurant? Somewhere I missed something. Something my cock can't feel. Even my heart can't feel. Something that keeps you from fucking while sharks are eating your neighbors; while one is coming for you. I broke the hearts of three wives. It's not what I set out to do. We were in bed, and there were all those fins. I ripped childhood from five children. It'll always be with them, that pain. Like joints that hurt when it rains. There's more to it, but I can't find it. It's not walking with a cane and giving cigar rings to grandchildren. You know anyone in AA?"

She nodded. Her eyes were damp, and he knew from them what his own face showed.

"You know that look they have when it's really behind them? When they've been dry for years? Like there's a part of them that nothing in the world can touch. Not pain. Not grief. Not even love. But where do I go for that? What street is it on? Where's the door?" He held the ashtray and sat up. "Where?" Looking at Doreen, he felt tears in his throat, then in his eyes and on his face. "I want that door," he said; then he could not speak. His stomach tightened, his body jerked forward, and his head bowed as he wept. She took the ashtray and cigarette from him and tightly held him with one arm, and with a hand she petted his cheek, pressing it against hers; she gently rocked him.

"You poor man," she said.

He knew what she felt, at the core of her tender voice and touch. He had held in his arms suffering women and children, knew that all anyone could do was hold and touch and speak, watch and listen, and wish the pain would end. Gratefully he leaned against her, moving with the push and pull of her arm. He could see nothing beyond this sorrow, could not imagine what he might say or do when it left him in Doreen's embrace.

The Last Moon

T HE MURDER BEGAN SOMEPLACE IN HER heart, a place she had never been: it was like a shadowed mountain pass, then a brilliant plain. The plain drew her. She stepped into it one night in bed with the sixteen-year-old boy. They lay naked in the dark room; it was late winter and cold still, and the light of streetlamps came through the windows. The boy held her; his breath was slowing now, and he pushed his hair away from his left eye. Soon he would be ready again. She was twenty-five; she was a guidance counselor at the only high school in town; her husband coached three sports. Now it was basketball, and he was thirty miles away, at a game.

She was on the bed she had chosen with her husband nineteen months ago, when they bought the house and began to buy things to put in it. They were engaged then, and they married a month later. Now she did not feel the bed holding her, or the room, the dead witness of its walls; she felt only her body, as when running early in the morning in this New England town where trees shaded lawns and the park and her office at school, she felt only her blood and muscles and breath, and not the earth her feet struck; as on the high diving board she felt only her gathered flesh, and not the board that held her above air and water. She said: "We could kill him."

Her voice, her words, seemed to stay in the air above their faces, as though, looking at the boy's eyes, she could reach up and with a finger touch each word. She could look at them; she could listen to her voice: it was low and strong, and slightly buoyant, enough so she could brush away the words, scatter them in the dark air, say she did not truly intend them; and in her tone was muted anticipation of the boy saying yes, and so taking the words from the air, making them part of his body, and of hers. The boy said: "Why?"

"I'd have the house. There's insurance on the mortgage. And another policy for two hundred thousand. We could do anything."

He believed her, and he would tell the detectives this, when they broke him; and he would say it on the witness stand, crying, looking again and again at his mother and father. He would tell it first on a warm spring afternoon to a boy who had been his friend since they were six; the boy would be horrified and, after days of pain, would tell his older brother, then his parents.

She was not lying about the house and the money,

but they were not the truth. The truth was in this place where she breathed and her heart beat as she lay in the boy's arms. She felt the boy's breath on her cheek, felt her own going out of her parted lips, and she could see how to do it. She could see him doing it, and she could see herself at that moment sitting in the café, drinking tea. She knew now that he would say yes. He had said "Why?" and he would say *How?* and then he would say yes, not with that word alone, but with many words. She would use many words, too; that is how they would plan it. She would talk about the house and the money, and where they could go with the money, when he was older, when he did not live at home; she would say: "We can make love in Spain." But she would never tell him where they were truly going. She would plead not guilty, and people would hear and read what the boy said about the house and the money. In prison she would tell the truth only to her pale and thin girlfriend, weeping as she told it, because she was young and smart, strong and pretty, and she was in prison forever.

In bed the boy stared; they had been lying in the dark long enough for her to see the light in his eyes. No naked girl had kindled this boy until she did. In her office, before she invited him to her house, his eyes were bright, as they were now: he sat in the chair in front of her desk and he could not look away from her; he looked at her hands on her desk, her shoulders beneath pale blue cotton, her blond hair, her mouth; he could not look at her eyes. This was in autumn, and she wanted his frenzy inside her. In bed that night in late winter, the skin of her face felt his eyes, as if their focused light were a point of warmth. He said: "He's really big."

"You could use a gun."

"I've never shot one."

"You'll be close. Can you get a gun?"

"My brother-in-law has some."

"You could take one. Then put it back."

"Where would he be?"

"In his car. You'll wait in the backseat. At night while they're playing a game on the road."

"What if guys are in the parking lot?"

"He does things in his office. He always goes home last. I'll give you a key. You'll take his money and his watch, and throw the watch in the river."

"Do you hate him?"

"He's just ordinary. I can do better."

The boy thought better meant him; she saw this in his eyes.

On the winter night of the murder, she sat in the café, at a table covered with a white cloth, and drank tea with a slice of lemon. She wore a brown sweater and jeans and hiking boots; her leather purse was on the table, and her dark blue parka hung on the back of the chair. She lifted the cup with her thumb and fore-finger, felt the solid curve of its handle, the heat of tea in her mouth and throat. She glanced at her watch, knowing the time before she saw the gold hands. She felt each second in her chest and stomach, faster than her breath, slower than her heart. She watched a gray-ing man and woman wearing sweaters and eating cake at a table; they put forks of cake in their mouths, look-ing at each other, as if they were speaking, or smiling. She watched the large and pleasant woman in a loose green blouse, sitting behind the counter and looking out the window, where people from the movie theater were on the sidewalk.

It would be soon now, the boys leaving the locker room, her husband in his blue suit and white shirt unbuttoned at the collar, the knot of his maroon tie pulled down from his throat, standing in the doorway of his office, talking to the boys as they left. In the car the boy lay waiting, the revolver warm in his hands, the boy afraid of failing and afraid of not failing, afraid of his parents and police and prison; but he was ablaze; he would do it. She watched two teenaged girls drinking Cokes at the counter, and saw the boy on the floor of the car and her husband at his desk in his office; they were inside her, in that place where she lived now.

This place would not have come to her if she had not taken the boy. Before she took him, she knew: even as she waited for him at her house on the first night, she knew that he was not what she wanted, that the boy and her desire were the form of something else she moved closer to when he rang the bell and she opened the door, and pulled him inside and closed the door, and locked it. People she knew, people she had always known, would call it passion, or happiness. They did not know. They were someplace behind her—they always were—and people like them came into the café now, moviegoers sitting at the counter and tables. She watched them. She had watched her husband, these days of snowfall and sunlight, these nights since the one when she said: "We could kill him," and in her heart then he was dead and she was in motion; and for the next eleven days and twelve nights she heard and saw him from that distance, and she made love with him because it was dazzling. The boy was behind her, too; she believed she would keep him for a while, and someday spit him out of her, return him to the place she watched herself watching now: people eating cake and sipping tea.

While beneath her fast heart, her husband left his office and the gymnasium, his gray overcoat unbuttoned, his head bare as he walked into the parking lot under his last moon. The boy lay in the dark and her husband opened the door, and dim light was in the car, and he got inside and closed the door, and it was dark again. The boy rose, and her husband's head and the revolver and the bullet and the boy were poised. In her body she saw the flash, heard the explosion of powder, saw the sudden hole and the spray of blood, her husband's dead eyes and falling face. Her hands rested on the table. It could be in this second; or the next; or the one a minute ago. Her right hand moved toward the cup, and she felt that her arm could reach through the night sky, her thumb and forefinger open to hold the moon.

The Timing of Sin

ON A THURSDAY NIGHT IN EARLY AUTUMN she nearly committed adultery, was within minutes of consummating it, or within touches, kisses; it was difficult to measure by time or by her mouth and tongue and hands, or by his. She made love with her husband, Ted Briggs, on Thursday night and Friday night and at first light Saturday morning, before her young children woke. Early Saturday afternoon, wearing sunglasses and sneakers, gray gym shorts and a blue tank top and blue nylon jacket, LuAnn Arceneaux kissed her children, the girls ten and eight and the boy six, and Ted, broad and bearded, standing with his cane in the kitchen; and carrying her purse, she went through the mudroom and walked down the long, curving driveway, a forty-three-year-old woman with dark skin and long black hair she wore this afternoon in a ponytail. She smelled the tall pines she walked past on her right, and the sunscreen she had rubbed on her face and arms and shoulders and legs. When she rounded the curve, she saw Marsha stopping her car in the road, then turning into the driveway, a Japanese car with dust on most of its red surface, and Marsha waving behind the windshield. LuAnn got into the car and they kissed cheeks.

They were talking about the lovely weather before Marsha backed onto the road; then she drove past trees with yellow leaves, and red ones, and Marsha said the river would be beautiful, in this light, with the leaves at its banks. Marsha's nylon jacket and shorts were silver, and LuAnn guessed she was wearing the purple tank top. Her hair was auburn, cut above her shoulders, and her sunglasses were dark. They lit cigarettes and LuAnn said they could just take beer to the park and lie in the sun, and Marsha said she could do that; her son, who was seven, had refused every morning this week to get out of bed, to dress, and to go to school, and she fought him as he dressed, and she and Bill and Annie encouraged him at breakfast, and snapped at him, and ordered him, and he went to school. LuAnn said that Julia and Elizabeth and Sam were good on school mornings; sometimes they fought with each other, but they did that in summer, too; and Marsha said if a workout didn't give her the same relief smoking and drinking did, she'd get a six-pack now; she said she had brought them a bottle of water. They were driving on a road built through a forest. LuAnn wondered if the road had once been a trail for loggers, for horse-drawn wagons and carriages. Large houses were acres apart, built on lawns surrounded by trees. LuAnn said: "Maybe something's wrong at school. A bully."

"I think he doesn't like the way I am in the morning. I don't like morning. Not on weekdays."

"We made love this morning."

"During cartoons?"

They drove out of the trees. There was a farm on the left, and beyond the dead cornstalks LuAnn saw the river; across the road from the farm were houses, and after the farm they were on both sides of the road. LuAnn said: "I woke up early."

"That's really good." Children were on the grass and sidewalks, cars were on the road, and men were mowing lawns. "If I *ever* woke up first, without the clock radio, I probably wouldn't even think of that. I'd creep to the kitchen and drink coffee and smoke cigarettes and stare. I work too Goddamned much."

"I don't miss it."

"I'm sick of it. I want your life. Or Ted's money. Imagine: in the morning. Ted will be a lamb all day. He'll take you to dinner."

"A stallion. When his day starts with sex, he sort of stays fixed on it."

"So you'll put on something pretty, go to Boston, have dinner."

"I feel like a movie. Some nice video the children can see."

"Get Zorro. Little girls love Zorro."

At an intersection Marsha stopped, waited for cars to pass, then turned left and drove a block between houses with small front lawns, and swaths of lawns or low wooden fences between them. There was a one-story yellow house with green trim and a maple with red leaves in the yard and a blue tricycle on the front porch; LuAnn imagined herself living in it; she loved her life and she knew she would love it in that yellow house, too. As a young woman working in Boston for an insurance company, then a small publisher, she had thought very little about money; then she had married Ted, a lawyer, and always there was plenty of money; so all her life she had not worried about it, except having so much of it; when she paid the monthly bills, she sent checks to homes for those who have no homes. On Thursday nights she went to a home for teenaged girls and read a story to some of them. It was not something she felt like leaving her house to do on Thursday nights; but she believed in sharing her gifts, and she liked the girls.

Just this summer she and Ted had bought the big house on the country road and she loved being in it, and was grateful for the money they had; it saved her from a job, and from some difficulties, and she had a housekeeper. She could live in the yellow house. She would miss looking out her windows at the rise and fall of wooded land, miss the solitude of trees, the private spaces her large house gave, and her big kitchen. But she knew that she and Ted, and Julia and Elizabeth and Sam, would be no different. She wished Marsha could quit her job. Marsha turned onto a narrow street and drove downhill, the red-brick hospital on their left, and farther down a yellow-brick church where LuAnn went to Mass. Marsha turned and drove past the church; they tossed their cigarettes out the windows, and went past the football stadium, and turned into a parking lot. The high school team was playing and through her open window LuAnn heard the band, and she looked at people sitting high in the stands. She and Marsha put their sunglasses on the dashboard, got out of the car, took off their jackets, and put them on the front seat, covering their purses. Marsha was wearing the purple top and holding her key ring. She came around the car and they started walking fast, across the lot and onto an asphalt path. To their right, black boys without shirts played basketball on a court. A woman on a bicycle rode toward them, and a young couple on Rollerblades came from behind them and skirted them and went bending and swaying up the slope. Large trees stood scattered in the park, and the high sun shone on the path and warmed LuAnn's face. She said: "I almost cheated Thursday night."

Marsha looked at her and said: "I wish I'd had the chance. Tell."

"You do?"

"I'm human. Depends on who it was."

The path gently rose and LuAnn looked at the trees on the riverbank and, far away, the trees across the river; she could not see the water.

"Roger Sibley," she said.

"Who's Roger Sibley?"

"The director. Of the girls' home."

"Him?"

"What's wrong with him?"

"Nothing. I saw him that one time, in the bar. The reason I said *him* was I couldn't get a picture. How do you get that done while you're reading—What?"

"Alice Munro."

"You look like you're in heat."

"I am. That's why this morning I—" She looked at Marsha's hazel eyes. "And last night and Thursday night. I'm burning it up with Ted."

In Marsha's eyes was a brief concupiscent light; then she smiled and looked ahead, and LuAnn did, and they walked between two old oaks with yellow leaves. The football crowd cheered and someone steadily beat a bass drum, and LuAnn heard her deep breath and Marsha's, in rhythm. Desire was part of their friendship and they had known it for a long time; known they could be lovers and they would not be; they neither talked about it nor avoided talking about it.

"Lucky Ted," Marsha said, and LuAnn looked at her in profile, at her mouth and a trickle of sweat on her cheek. "I'm going to volunteer there. You're sitting in a room with some very unlucky girls, you're reading Alice Munro, and somehow—" LuAnn saw the room, and Sylvie, sixteen, with a small body and a pretty face and light brown hair down to her lower back and falling over her cheek when she lowered her head; Sylvie watching, listening to LuAnn read. "Didn't you tell me it was a glass room?"

"It's all windows—the upper halves of the walls. It's on the first floor, and it doesn't open to the outside. You can't be in there without someone seeing you. It was later, in my car."

"Holy shit."

"It's their smoking room—the girls, the staff. The girls can smoke on the sundeck, if a woman is with them. They can't be alone. Only in the bathroom or when they go to bed. Sometimes when I'm reading, girls come in to smoke, and sometimes they stay and listen to the rest of the story; sometimes they just listen while they're smoking, then leave. Thursday I had my regular four—anyone can come; I wish they all would—but I had Sylvie and Tracy and Lisa and Annette. Sylvie is smart. They've all seen too much and heard too much, and they've had too much done to them, and they've done too much. Some don't seem bright, but I don't know if that's because they've spent all their lives surviving, or if they wouldn't be bright anyway. But Sylvie is smart. If she had just had ordinary parents—" LuAnn saw again the small yellow house in the neighborhood near the hospital. "Just ordinary, bumbling, mistaken parents, who loved her and made a home for her, and fed her, and sent her to school. Read her a story at bedtime. Talked to her. She'd be in high school in some little town, with girl-friends, and a boyfriend, and learning to drive, and thinking about college. What she got was a father she's never seen and a mother whose boyfriends fucked her since she was four years old. There was always some-body fucking her till she was twelve; then she ran away and everybody fucked her. She was on the streets till she got in drug trouble. Then it was juvenile court, and now she's watched all the time, and fed, and taught. And loved, too. By some of the girls, and the staff."

"And you."

"And me. Sometimes I think about adopting her. But I don't know if I have it in me. She was the catalyst Thursday night."

The path rose toward the riverbank; then she could see the water. On her right, a Hispanic family with three young children sat on the grass, eating sand-wiches. To her left were trees, tall and close to one an-other, their leaves red and yellow. In the stadium the band played. The river was bright blue and moving toward the sea. The path turned away from the trees and was flat, parallel to the river, and the couple on Rollerblades came toward them, and LuAnn and Marsha parted to let them through. Trees lined the high bank and LuAnn looked between their trunks at the river, and across it at red and golden trees, and hills.

"Sylvie asked if she could go to the bathroom. I stopped reading. She took her purse. I lit a cigarette. So did the girls. We talked about our hair. Tracy had hers cut, and she dyed it pink. Some girls were doing homework at tables in the dining room. A staff woman was with them—Sherri—reading something. Roger was working in his office. Facing me, but his head was down; he was doing something at his desk. I looked at his yellow rusty hair. I finished my cigarette. The girls finished theirs. We were still talking about hair and I was looking around through the glass, and then Annette was, and I said to her: 'Do you think Sylvie's all right?' And Lisa and Tracy stopped talking, and Annette said: 'I don't know.' And she sounded like she did know. Or she sounded frightened. She's Sylvie's roommate. And Tracy and Lisa and Annette looked at me; there was trouble in their eyes, and they were waiting. For me. For Sylvie. For what was going to happen next in their lives. So I said: 'I'll just check on her,' and I left my purse on the floor by my chair, and while I was going through the dining room, and girls were looking up from their homework and saying hi, and I was smiling and saying hi, I worried about the money in my purse, but it wasn't really the money; it was having it taken from my purse, my intimate piece of dead calf, and I was feeling stupid for leaving that temptation for three girls who have so many good reasons to take from somebody, especially some foolish woman with money who reads to them so she can believe or just feel that she's doing *some*thing for the hopeless—"

"You Catholics can be very complicated."

"We're good at sin. We study it."

"Did they take your cash?"

"No."

"If they had, would it be your sin?"

"Equally." She smiled. "At least. But mostly I was worried about Sylvie. She hadn't looked sick. She has these pink cheeks. I went down the hall to the bathroom and knocked on the door. It was quiet. I was alone in the hall, and I knocked again, and it was still quiet. So I said her name. Then I said it again, and knocked. Then I said it louder; then I went fast through the dining room and past the glass room, and Lisa and Annette and Tracy watched me, and I tapped on Roger's window. When he looked up and saw my face, he got up fast. He's so big, but he's quick. And he always looks calm. He's not. You look at his eyes and you know he's con*tained*. He opened the door and I told him and he nodded—just that—and was past me, walking as fast as we are now, and I followed him, and I'm sure the girls' eyes did, in the glass room and the dining room; I was only looking at his back I couldn't see around and his head I couldn't see over, and I noticed he was quiet, his shoes—his feet—didn't make a sound, and he turned down the hall and stopped at the bathroom and knocked lightly. Then he spoke very softly. So very softly. He said: 'Sylvie?' and I imagined being Sylvie in there, hearing him. Probably she never heard a man speak so softly till she met Roger. Not with love, any-

way. He said: 'Sylvie, open the door, please.' Then two
of the staff came, Susan and Deborah, and they called
Sylvie. Roger said: 'Sylvie. Sylvie, I'll have to open the
door.' I was standing beside him. He opened the door,
and she was standing there with her sleeves pushed up
to her elbows, she was wearing a teal sweater, and she
was stabbing her wrist with a ballpoint, her left wrist,
and she had stabbed her hand; it was bleeding and her
wrist was, not a lot, but she was raising the pen high
and *stab*bing—" LuAnn raised her right fist and swung
it down to her left and turned it back and forth—"and
twisting the pen in her flesh, and that's what she was
looking at when Roger opened the door. She looked up
at us. Not at any one of us. I know she saw us all, but
her eyes—those big sweet brown eyes—saw something
else, maybe saw the pen going in, or the pen when she
held it high and drove it down. Maybe she saw her
whole self, stabbing, being pierced. As if she stood beside herself and watched. Maybe what she stared at was
just being alone. This was an instant, that look in her
eyes. Then Roger moved and grabbed her hand with
the pen, and Susan was behind her, holding her waist,
and Deborah was holding her bleeding arm and turning her to the sink. Sylvie was fighting. I just stood in
the doorway, the woman who reads. I know she saw
me. But seeing me wasn't in her eyes. She was bucking,
squirming, elbowing, kicking. And the sound she made
was a long moan. It was plaintive, and it was angry,
and her head was moving, up and down when she
bucked and kicked, side to side when she squirmed and
elbowed, and all the time she made this loud sound of
despair; it only paused when/she inhaled, but it was so
loud and she was in so much pain that it didn't even

seem to pause; it was like she was blowing a trumpet to raise the devil. I was trembling."

"Jesus. I couldn't do that work."

"I don't. It was like an accident in my life."

"I mean the staff. This must happen and happen."

"It does. I've only heard about it, till Thursday."

The trail ended at a parking lot, and between it and the river were picnic tables. Teenaged girls and boys were sitting on one, and a family sat at another with food. Marsha said: "You want to walk on the road?"

"Yes," LuAnn said, her arms swinging, sweat dripping on her skin, her tank top damp, her leg muscles warm with blood, and eager, her breath deep, and her biceps hard, her wrists and hands relaxed. Beyond the parking lot was a road going upriver. They walked through shadows of pines; then were on the road, and around a curve, and LuAnn could not hear the crowd at the stadium. They walked on the side of the road, with the river on their left and houses on their right. There were no cars; probably few people used the road, except those who lived on it. The river sparkled. Marsha said: "You believe in the devil?"

"I don't know. I believe in possessions, and exorcisms. I don't know if there's a devil. I used to think of Christ in the desert, tempted by this powerful, visible, evil spirit. Maybe ugly with horns and fur, maybe beautiful, a shining face with black eyes. Now I think what tempted Him was his humanity. He was hungry. He wanted people to know who He was. He wanted to just take over and call the shots. Impose agâpe on everyone. It's funny, when I was at BU, somebody in our group started this: if you said the Lord's Prayer backward, the devil would appear. There were probably only two of us who even believed in God. Me, and one of the guys. We laughed, we snorted coke, we drank tequila, but no one would say that prayer backward. I wouldn't right now. I don't know if there's a devil, and I'll stay with that."

"We hardly need him."

"No. We're doing fine on our own. Sylvie cried. Deborah was washing her. That's when she stopped that awful moan; her eyes had been dry, and bright with *some*thing that was in her, and when Deborah ran water on her arm, she cried, deep, loud crying, and the tears jumped out of her eyes; her face was wet, and Deborah was washing and blood was in the sink, but it stopped soon, the bleeding; Sylvie quit fighting as soon as she cried. She looked like she'd fall down if they weren't holding her. Roger just kept saying her name, and he loosened his grip on her right arm; then he let it go, and she clutched him, his sleeve, then his bare arm. There she was, in her jeans and teal sweater, sobbing. She was looking at Roger, but I don't think she can remember what his face was like then, in the bathroom. Maybe his touch, his voice. She was still seeing herself, her pain. She's in a hospital now. Psychiatric. After a while she'll go back to the home. And after a while she'll say she's sorry, that she did it to get attention. She'll even say it to me, one Thursday night. And it's bullshit. She did it because hurting her body felt better than the pain in her soul, and it gave her relief."

"Sure it does. I used to binge, when I was a girl. I still do."

"With food?" She looked at Marsha, who was smiling and wiping sweat from her brow.

"Not now. I go to the gym. I work on those machines

till I'm not me anymore. In the shower I'm me again, but the part of me I couldn't stand is dead. It's in the gym, draped over a Universal."

The road curved with the river, climbed and curved again, and a speedboat came downriver and LuAnn watched its wake spreading. Its motor was the only sound in the air. Then it was gone, and she said: "When Ted got hurt, he was relieved. After the explosion, when he was on the ground and there were no more explosions and he knew he was alive. His captain was talking to him and a corpsman was working on his leg, and he knew he was alive and he was going home, and he was relieved. He said it took him months, when he got out of the hospital in Philadelphia, to know it wasn't relief he felt. It was gratitude. Because it was over, for him. He was going home. He had been afraid every day and every night at Khe Sanh, but it wasn't that. He said sometimes the fear was a rush. It was the pain in his soul. It's still there. All those boys he bandaged and shot up with morphine, talked to while they died or didn't die, boys he saved or didn't, all the boys whose bleeding he stopped and whose shock he stopped, and they went home without arms or legs or with their cocks and balls shredded. When he got hit, his pain was terrible, but he had morphine. I think Sylvie felt something on the edge of that. In its penumbra. But she's not in a war she can come home from. When I talk to Ted about these girls, what they say about their lives, what the staff tells me, he says he'd rather Vietnam than a childhood of being raped by people he was born to trust. Nobody he trusted hurt him over there, and he always felt loved. Sylvie kept crying—her face was on Roger's chest—and Deborah bandaged the cuts, and I looked behind me, and the hall was full of girls and three staff, talking to them, turning them around, getting them out of the hall. Susan went through them, to call the hospital. Roger and Deborah were holding Sylvie, and they started walking her toward me, or toward the doorway I stood in, and I backed up, looking at Sylvie. Tears were still on her face, but she was quiet. She was breathing through her mouth; I could hear it. I looked at Roger. He was watching Sylvie and his face was firm and gentle at the same time. He was a *fa*ther, doing what he could, and I knew he was sad and disappointed; maybe he felt betrayed, hopeless, but none of that showed, and I just wanted to lean against the wall and cry. I've never seen a child hurt herself on purpose. Or an adult, either; not violently, just drugs and drinking and smoking and eating—"

"And working."

"Yes."

"You were helpless, too." Ducks were sitting on the river, gently bobbing. "If it were Julia or Elizabeth, you'd have been different."

LuAnn looked at her.

"You're right. I haven't thought of that. I just felt in the way. So I got out of the way. I turned and went down the hall and through the dining room, and didn't look at anyone. All the girls were standing in the dining room, with Sherri and another woman. I went to the glass room and sat down. Annette and Lisa and Tracy hadn't come back, and their purses were gone. Roger and Deborah came with Sylvie and walked her through the dining room, with everybody watching. Annette and a woman came from the bedrooms.

Annette was carrying an overnight bag, and she handed it to Deborah; then she and the woman stood with the others. Roger and Deborah took Sylvie through the kitchen and outside. The girls were moving tables and putting chairs in a circle, and then I knew they were going to have a meeting now, to talk about it. So I went outside. Roger was standing in the driveway, and Susan was starting the van, and Deborah was holding the passenger door for Sylvie, and she got in with her bag, and Deborah sat beside her. I stood on the steps, looking past Roger at Sylvie. When they backed out, I started to wave. My arm started to; but I didn't let it. Then they were gone, and Roger stood looking at the road. He folded his arms. He thought he was alone. I've always had a crush on him, since I started there—"

"You didn't tell *me* that."

"A crush. I have them all the time. I have one on the guy who delivers springwater."

"You, too?"

"We have the same guy?"

"I had an affair with one. It ended my first marriage."

They stopped and looked at each other. LuAnn said: "That's why it ended, and you never told me?"

"It was eighteen years ago, and it was dramatic and tragic and all that. Now it seems like another life."

They turned and walked downriver, LuAnn watching Marsha, trying to see her eighteen years ago. Marsha said: "This is my real marriage. With Bill and Annie and Stephen. Rick and I didn't last two years. We were young, and it was before AIDS, and I wasn't used to monogamy. You remember."

"I was mostly sequential, except in college."

"I was multiple. Then I was married, and I didn't want children yet, and Rick was light-years from it. I've rewritten that marriage so much in my head that it's not real anymore. I know I loved him, and he loved me; after that, I don't know what we were doing. This cute, sexy guy delivered water early in the morning—usually Rick was in the shower or shaving—and I made some moves and he made some moves, and one morning he kissed me. I told him to come back in an hour, and Rick left for work—he had to drive farther than I did—then I called in sick. And stood in the living room and looked out the window for an hour, and bam, on the dot, here came the truck up my drive. After that we got on an adultery schedule. Rick was on the road a lot, and Derek would come to my house after work. It was winter, so it was dark early. He was married, too. He'd show up in his uniform, with all those muscles from carrying water. Here's what's odd: everything was fast. I don't think he was ever with me for two hours. But Rick caught us. He was on the road—in the air, really—selling in Chicago; it was a Tuesday night, and he was supposed to come home Wednesday. But he finished in Chicago a day early, and he didn't call; he just flew to Boston and got in his car, poor man, and drove home. I heard the door open. Because the bedroom door was open, and if it hadn't been, he would have walked in on us. But I heard the door—I don't know *how;* maybe when you're cheating you keep waiting for that door—and I told Derek to get dressed and I left him and closed the bedroom door, and ran down the hall just when Rick turned into it, still carrying his suitcase and briefcase, still in his overcoat—"

"You were naked?"

"I was naked." She smiled at LuAnn, then looked up at the sky. "I've thought about it over the years. Wondered if I meant to hurt him more. But I don't think so. I was never trying to hurt him, anyway. I may have had time to slip on my underpants, maybe my shirt—run down the hall, trying to button. But I don't think so. It was a small place, one story of a duplex. If *Ted* came home like that, you'd have time to get the guy down the back stairs, and dress and make the bed. 'Course you wouldn't hear him come in, either; you'd hear him on the stairs."

"What did Rick do?"

"I said: 'You can't come in. Somebody's here.' He said: 'Somebody's here?' He said it quietly, like we were conspirators. And he was conspiring with me, not about what I had been doing but about what he and I were doing right then, at that moment. He had made a decision: he wasn't going down the hall to confront, or to fight—"

"I would."

"I wouldn't be able not to. He was. He wasn't angry yet. Oh God, he was hurt. He put down his suitcase and briefcase. He kept looking at me. Tears were in his eyes; his mouth was open. Then he turned to leave. He took one step and stopped, and turned back to me again, and he looked at me that way. He picked up his suitcase and briefcase, looking at me. Then he walked out. His head was down; I watched him, and his head was down. At the back door he had to put down his suitcase and briefcase, to open it. I wanted to go pick them up, hold them for him while he opened the damned door; but I saw it in my head, and it looked like a cruel thing to do. It would look cruel. He opened the door and lifted the things through it and put them on the step. Then he went through and closed the door. I stood there and listened to his car starting and backing out and turning in the street. Then I went to the horrible bedroom, and Derek was dressed, his uniform coat, his gloves, and he looked as bad as Rick. I'm sure I did, too. But Derek's bad was fear. If he's stayed married, and he kept cheating, I think he goes to motels. I got dressed. I could not put on clothes fast enough. I said: 'That was Rick.' I said: 'You better go.' He just kept nodding his head. That man was already ten miles away, standing in my bedroom. He pecked me on the mouth, and was gone. Rick checked into a motel and called me. He wasn't angry yet. That came later. But from the *in*stant I heard him open that door, I paid for my fun. Paid and paid. Rick came back to the house once, to get his things. Derek brought water. We'd shake hands. He was nice and all. He'd ask how I was doing, say he was sorry. I'd look at him, and it didn't seem real. There was Derek past and Derek present, and Marsha past and Marsha present, and I felt *noth*ing exciting for him. Just this shared mis*take*. Regret. Then he'd leave with the empty bottles, and I'd drive to work and get on with other things. You know something that I'll never know?"

The road straightened and LuAnn saw the park, and heard shouting from the stadium.

"I'll never know if Rick and I would've made it. I loved him, there weren't any rules, or I didn't have any, I trusted my IUD, and I was just having fun. I never thought I could do so much damage. Because I never thought I'd get caught. So. I'm glad I'm with Bill. And if I were still with Rick, I wouldn't have Annie and Stephen. Maybe other children, but not Annie and Stephen. And Rick has children, and a wife he can probably trust, and loads of money. Still: if he hadn't come home early, or he'd called first, my fun with Gunga Din would have dried, and maybe I'd still be married to Rick. I tried to stay married to him. I begged, I promised, but I had broken his heart, and there was no way it would mend. Not with this woman, anyway." She looked at LuAnn. "I said I wished I'd had the chance Thursday night. That's all I meant. I hope I never cheat."

They moved into the pine shadows and onto the parking lot. A man with silver hair sat alone at a picnic table, reading a book. LuAnn said: "I didn't know I would till Thursday. I knew I could. Lots of times. With pleasure. But I knew I wouldn't. That was the trap: that I believed I knew I wouldn't." She looked at Marsha's eyes. "If you ever hear me say I know I won't do something, be gentle, okay?" Marsha smiled. "But love me, slap me." She looked past Marsha at the river; in the stadium, people cheered, someone beat the bass drum, rolled snare drums, and struck cymbals together. "Sex is like the weather. It's just there. One summer afternoon you drive to the mall, shop inside, go out again, and water is falling from the sky. It was blue when you went in, and now it's gray and water is falling, and you're wearing shorts and a T-shirt. There was a bright moon and a streetlamp down the road. I was standing on the steps, looking at Roger's hair in the light. He didn't move. So I went down the steps and on the driveway and he heard me and turned. When I got close, I could see his sorrow: in his cheeks, his mouth, his eyes.

He said: 'LuAnn.' I wanted to hold him tight, in his sorrow. He said: 'Are you all right?' and I said: 'Shaken. How are you?' He said he was tired. His voice was a sigh. I told him I didn't know how he stood it—he works sixty, seventy hours a week—and I asked if he thought Sylvie would be all right, would ever really be all right, and he said: 'I don't know.' Then he looked down and said: 'She's *got* to.' The front lawn there is deep and my car was parked beside the road, behind a row of lilacs. I looked at its roof and said: 'Are you going to the meeting?' and he said: 'Not right away. Sherri's running it,' and we started walking to my car. I got in and opened the window and he leaned down to it, looking at me, and I looked away to get my cigarettes. He said: 'Could I have one?' I opened my mouth to say sure, but the image that came was us sitting in the car, smoking; I said: 'Join me.' Before he got to the passenger door, I was feeling that first wave of thrill. Oh, *thrill* is dangerous; living is dangerous. He filled the seat. I gave him a cigarette and a light and lit mine. He's divorced and isn't with his children enough; he doesn't go home to them and wake up with them. He takes them on weekends, but sometimes he doesn't have whole weekends; the home takes him—girls run away or try to kill themselves, or some staff have the flu. So he hurts. He's one of those who hurts and just keeps going. There was a tree between us and the streetlamp in front of my car, and the road was lit, but we were in shadows there, and the lilacs between us and the home are tall, and I couldn't see the downstairs windows. There were houses across the street with lights low, people watching television. You could make love on their front lawns and they wouldn't know. Murder

somebody, and they wouldn't know till morning. I
wanted to kiss him and I was trying to think of something to say, about Sylvie, about *any*thing. Three drags
on my cigarette. Two or three on his. Then he said: 'I
like watching you read.' I didn't say anything; it was in
my face, though. Probably since he got in the car like
a panther, if panthers were shaped like bears. Probably
since I said: 'Join me.' He leaned to kiss me and I
leaned, and we were kissing and I reached behind him
and dropped my cigarette out his window, and I felt
him drop his. Then our hands were free: shirts unbuttoned. I was wearing jeans; we pulled them down and
my underpants, and his. I wanted to get in the passenger seat, with him kneeling on the floor and my feet on
the dashboard. I said: 'Move.' He pushed the seat back,
got a condom from his wallet, and took off his shoes
and slacks and shorts, and I was pushing my underpants and jeans—I had them to my ankles; then I knew
I couldn't. I wouldn't. Because of those seconds when
we weren't kissing and touching. I was touching my
jeans and my pants and my skin. I saw myself walking
into my house. I saw myself walking through the
kitchen and the dining room to Ted in the living room.
I didn't see Ted. Or Julia and Elizabeth and Sam in
their beds. I saw my face and the front of my body,
walking toward—me. Walking on the floor toward me.
And I knew I must not do this. I wanted to. All I could
feel was my body and this thing in my chest that
wanted to explode. Into blossom. But I knew, and I
pulled on my underpants and I was pulling up my jeans
and feeling with my feet for my moccasins, all that
breathing in the car, and I said: 'I can't.' I looked at
him. I hadn't stopped looking at him, but I looked

at his eyes and said: 'I'm sorry.' I had my jeans up and my moccasins on and by the time I was buttoning my shirt, he was dressed. His eyes were beautiful. He said: 'Don't be.'

"Then you know what? I had one clear thought: What's the difference between stopping now and going through with it? And it seemed right. Not the question, but the answer that was already in the question. There's no difference; that's what I felt, this great pull just to kiss him and get it done. We were still breathing hard. I said: 'I have to go.' He said: 'I understand.' He looked like he wanted to kiss me good night, hug me, maybe just a little kiss; I shook my head. He got out and shut the door and lowered his face to the window. I said: 'I'll see you Thursday.' He nodded, and I said: 'I'll see you carefully.' 'I won't bother you,' he said. Some of them think you're dormant till they kiss you. I said: 'I know.' I buckled the seat belt and started the car. He said: 'Good night, LuAnn.' He said it sweetly. I said: 'Good night' while I was shifting gears; then I drove. I looked in the mirror. He was standing by the road, watching. I stuck my arm out and waved. He waved. The road curved and I couldn't see him anymore and I drove home."

"Intact."

The path turned and LuAnn looked at the light on the river, then the trees on her right, and shadows on the ground beneath them and sunlight on fallen brown leaves. Then she looked ahead, at the stadium and the park.

"I guess so." She looked at Marsha. "Would you say intact?"

"Yes. That's what the struggle was about."

"It's still going on."

"No smoking in the car."

"No."

In the stadium the music was joyful and LuAnn walked to its beat. They passed the boys playing basketball, and she said: "I'll go to confession today."

"Really?"

"It's at four on Saturdays."

"I didn't know you did that."

"Not much."

"Do you think you need to?"

"Yes."

"To be forgiven?"

"No. I'm always being forgiven. But I'll get strength from it. We do it face-to-face now. I'll just go sit with the priest and tell him."

"If you tell him like you told me, you'll have another struggle on your hands."

"It's a very simple language. I'll say I placed myself in the occasion of sin, and I nearly committed adultery, and I don't want that to happen, ever."

"So you rehearse it?"

"I did, driving home Thursday night."

They came to the parking lot and slowed their pace, then stopped and turned around and stood watching the boys play. Marsha said: "That's it? What will the priest say?"

"Not much. Tell me to do something, and absolve me."

"Penance?"

"Not on my knees for hours. He'll probably tell me to spend a few minutes with God, asking for help. I'll be talking to you, too."

Marsha held LuAnn's shoulder, looked at her eyes.
"Do not *ev*er tell Ted."

"No. It wasn't him in the car. And why ever tell him there was a time when there wasn't him? There wasn't even Julia and Elizabeth and Sam; there was just me. It was the jeans that saved me. If I had been wearing a skirt I could've just pulled up. There wouldn't have been those seconds when I was only touching my own skin. And you can't be saved by jeans. So it was God, grace; and I don't think of Him with eyes, glancing away from all the horror and seeing what I was doing and stopping me before He turned away again to look aghast at the world. I don't know how it happens."

Marsha lowered her hand and smiled.

"Some people would just say you were being good."

"What I was being was hot. If I take all the credit for getting out of it, I have to take all the blame for getting into it, too. That's too simple, and too unbearable. My job is to try, and to be vigilant, and keep hoping. I need my jacket, and some water."

They turned and walked to the car.

At Night

S HE ALWAYS KNEW SHE WOULD BE A WIDOW; why, even before she was a bride, when she was engaged, she knew, in moments when she imagined herself very old, saw herself slow and lined and gray in a house alone, with photographs of children and grandchildren on a mantel over the fire. It was what women did, and she glimpsed it, over the years, as she glimpsed her own death. She had the children and the grandchildren, and some of the grandchildren moved to other states, but most of them stayed, and all her children did, close enough to visit by car, and they came to her, too, and filled her little house. The photographs hung in the bedroom and in the hall, and were on the mantel above the fireplace.

She was seventy-seven and her husband was, too,

and by now she had buried her parents and his, and a sister, and two of his brothers, and so many friends; and that had begun in her thirties, burying friends who were taken young. So she knew death was inside of her, inside him, too; something in her body would change—would stumble and fall, or stop, or let go; and something in his would. She did not want to lie helpless in bed for a long time, in pain, and she did not want him to, but she knew it was the way: you went to a doctor because of some trouble your body couldn't leave behind; then you were in the hospital; then you came home and took medicine and died.

Her life ending worried her very little, for here she was each morning, with him; he was long retired from the post office, and they ate breakfast and went for a walk in good weather, sometimes even in the cold when one of their sons shoveled the driveway and the sidewalk and poured rock salt so they wouldn't slip and fall and break a bone; and they went to the children and grandchildren, and the children and grandchildren came to them, and there was the house to keep, and the cooking, and their garden, and friends for a visit. They had plots in the cemetery and she knew everything that had to be done. She had four children, and when she called them with news, she started with the firstborn, then the next, and so on to the last; and this is how she planned to phone them, after she called the doctor, when whatever was coming to her husband came. Then she would watch as in the hospital bed and then in their bed he shrank and died, and near the end the family would all gather to see him alive. Then he would not be, and she would be alone in the house, with the telephone and the car and the children coming to see her.

But on the summer night when he died while she slept, probably while he slept, too, she woke in the cool dark, the windows open and a pale light in the sky, and the birds singing, and she knew before she turned to him, and she did not think of her children, or of being alone. She rolled toward him and touched his face, and her love went out of her, into his cooling skin, and she wept for what it had done to him, crept up and taken him while he slept and dreamed. Maybe it came out of a dream and the dream became it. Wept, lying on her side, with her hand on his cheek, because he had been alone with it, surprised, maybe confused now as he wandered while the birds sang, seeing the birds, seeing her lying beside his flesh, touching his cheek, saying: "Oh hon—"

Out of the Snow

ON A DARK WINTER MORNING, UPSTAIRS IN her new home, LuAnn woke to classical piano on the clock radio; she was in her forty-fourth year, she had a few strands of gray in her long black hair, and this was her eighty-third day without smoking; before opening her eyes she remembered dreaming in the night of a red-and-white package of cigarettes. Then she looked at Ted limping naked to the closet. He was a big man; the sideburns of his brown beard were gray. His knee had been shattered and torn by shrapnel when he was nineteen in Vietnam, and it would not completely bend, and often it was painful. She turned off the radio, and in the silence she could feel her children sleeping; it was as though she heard their breath and saw their faces on pillows. She stood, wearing a white gown, and started to make the bed, and Ted in his burgundy robe came to help, and she remembered last night's lovemaking, and watched him smoothing the blue satin comforter. She said: "I dreamed of cigarettes last night."

"That isn't fair."

"I'd love one now, with coffee."

"So would I."

"Great. Is that why I'm doing this? So eighteen years from now I'll want to smoke?"

His blue eyes watched her. That is what he did most of the time, when she was angry or sad or frightened: watched her and listened. He had told her he stopped believing in advice years before he met her, or stopped believing people wanted advice; they wanted to be looked at and heard by someone who loved them. She said: "Nice night, Ted."

"Yes." He smiled. "Nice night, LuAnn."

He went to the bathroom at the far end of the hall, and she went to the one she shared with Julia and Elizabeth. She put on makeup, and in the bedroom she dressed in jeans and a green turtleneck and high black boots. Then she went to the children's rooms and woke them by placing a hand on their shoulders: Julia, her first child, who was ten, then Elizabeth, then Sam, lying among stuffed bears. She always woke them gently because she felt she was pulling them from childhood. They were dark-haired, sleepy, and slow to dress. She knew they were slow because they were reluctant, but there was something more, something she wanted to acquire; they were slow in summer, too, dressing for the beach. Hurry was imposed on them by adults; they had not lived long enough to see time as something they

should control, long enough to believe they could. Lu-
Ann had taken maternity leave to give birth to Julia,
and had not gone back to her job. She had been the
publicity director of a small publisher in Boston. Two
years later Elizabeth was born, and after another two
Sam, and by then LuAnn knew what these children
knew: they ate when they were hungry, slept when they
were tired, and looked at the present with curiosity. She
was trying to focus on the present now, as she went
downstairs, aware of her breathing, her leg muscles, the
smell of coffee, the electric light in the dining room and
twilight in the living room; and wanting to smoke, then
calling over her shoulder to the children to hurry.

In the kitchen, Ted stood with his cane, pouring
coffee; he wore his blue double-breasted suit and a red
tie with a pale blue shirt. He was flying to Baltimore to
take a deposition and would stay there for the night.
He had brought in the newspaper from the box at the
end of their long driveway that curved downhill
through trees. He put a spoon of sugar and some hot
milk from a pot in her coffee, then handed it to her. He
stood resting on his cane as she took her first sip; then
with a finger he touched her knuckles at the handle of
the cup, and bent down and gave her a quick kiss; his
throat and his cheeks above his beard smelled of
aftershave lotion, and she breathed that with the aroma
of coffee and said: "You're not bad, Ted Briggs."

"Neither are you, Ms. Arceneaux."

She went through the mudroom, where boots were
on benches and coats hung on pegs, and stepped outside, and smelled snow in the air. The evergreens were
still black and the sky was dark gray. She breathed

deeply into her stomach and looked up at the sky and raised her arms. She went back into the light of the kitchen; upstairs the children's steps were slow but steady, so she did not call to them. Ted was making sandwiches at the counter. She took three grapefruit from the refrigerator and stood beside him and sliced the grapefruit in halves, then cut their sections from the rind. She drank coffee and poured measuring cups of water into a pot. Until eighty-three days ago she had waked herself each morning for twenty-six years with coffee and cigarettes. Her flesh could not remember what it had felt, waking without wanting those. She stepped to the sink and poured out her coffee, then spread butter on eight slices of bread, and margarine on two. Ted's cholesterol was high, and she obeyed the rules about that, and imposed them on him; she ate what she wanted to, and she did not give margarine to the children because she did not trust it, suspecting that decades from now it would attack them in ways no one had predicted. She sprinkled brown sugar on the bread, then cinnamon, and looked at Ted's profile and said: "You could cheat tonight, you know. Have yourself a great dinner."

"I plan to."

She wondered if she had really been talking about food, then knew that she was, and it had reminded her of adultery. Once she had nearly cheated, and she had learned how simple and even negligible it could be, making love with someone else while loving your husband; and since then she had known it could happen to Ted, as easily as a tire blowing out, or a bluefish striking his hook. She had told none of this to him; she had told Marsha and had confessed to a priest that in her heart she had been unfaithful, though not with her body.

He sliced the sandwiches in triangular halves, wrapped them in waxed paper, and placed them in the three lunch boxes. They were red, blue, yellow. He wrapped cookies and put in each box an apple and a tangerine. She imagined him tonight eating pâté and duck, and herself in the living room, after the children were asleep, smoking cigarettes. She looked at the clock and was about to call the children, knowing her voice would be high and tense, but then she heard them on the stairs. They came into the dining room, Julia and Elizabeth murmuring, Sam gazing, seeing something in his mind that was nowhere in the room. She quietly marveled at these little people: they were dressed; they wore shoes; their hair was brushed. Probably their beds were made. She sat with them and Ted and ate grape-fruit. Then she boiled the water in the pot, measured oatmeal into it, and watched it boil again, then lowered the flame. She slid the pan of cinnamon bread into the oven, left the door partially open, and turned on the broiler.

Her mind was eluding her: it was living the day ahead of her; it was in the aisle of the supermarket, it was bringing the groceries into the house and putting them away; it was driving to the gym for aerobics and weight training; it was home eating lunch, then taking clothes to the dry cleaners and getting the clothes that were there, and driving home before three-forty when the school bus brought the children to the driveway; it was lighting charcoal in the grill on the sundeck. Maybe snow would be falling then; she loved cooking in the snow. She had a housekeeper three days a week and she liked running the household. None of it absorbed her fully enough to imprison her mind, as some work in school and some at the publishing house had. So freedom was both her challenge and her vocation: she was free on most days and nights to concentrate fully on the moment at hand, and this was far more difficult than performing work she had been assigned as a student for sixteen years, and a worker for eleven. She had told Ted she must learn to be five again, before time began to mean what one could produce in its passing; or to be like St. Thérèse of Lisieux, who knew so young that the essence of life was in the simplest of tasks, and in kindness to the people in your life. Watching the brown sugar bubbling in the light of the flames, smelling it and the cinnamon, and listening to her family talking about snow, she told herself that this toast and oatmeal were a sacrament, the physical form that love assumed in this moment, as last night's lovemaking was, as most of her actions were. When she was able to remember this and concentrate on it, she knew the significance of what she was doing; as now, using a pot holder, she drew the pan from the oven, then spooned oatmeal into bowls her family came from the dining room to receive from her hands.

At seven forty-five the children put on parkas and gloves; Sam wore a ski cap, and the girls kept theirs in their pockets. They carried book bags and lunch boxes and LuAnn and Ted went outside with them, kissed them, and watched them walking down the dark asphalt drive, till it curved around pines and they were out of sight. She cleared the table and Ted rinsed things and put them in the dishwasher. He went upstairs, then came down wearing a dark blue overcoat, his cane in his right hand, his left holding a small suitcase and his briefcase. She took the briefcase and, without a coat, carried it out to his car in the garage and said: "Call me."

"I will."

"I hate airplanes."

"It'll be fine."

Two images pierced her: Ted in a plane above the earth, and Julia, Elizabeth, and Sam disappearing in the gray light as they rounded the pine trees. She said: "There's so much to fear."

"I know. And we've been lucky."

"I've been thanking God for fear."

"You have?"

"This winter. One afternoon the bus was late with the children. My imagination was like a storm. I stood at the road, and I couldn't get rid of all the terrible pictures. So I started thanking God for this fear, because it meant I love them so much. The sun was shining on the snow and pines, and I stood down there, thinking of what it would be like not to have that fear; not to love anyone so much that you couldn't imagine living on the earth without them." She shivered from the cold, and he held her; her lips were at his throat and she said: "I looked at all that beauty around me, and I was grateful. I was still afraid, but the worst of it went out of me."

He was pressing her against his broad, firm chest. He cried easily and she knew tears were in his eyes now. She kissed him, then stood hugging herself for warmth as he got into the car and backed out of the garage, turning and heading downhill. Before the curve, he waved his arm out the window, and she raised hers; then he was gone.

She went inside, put an Ella Fitzgerald compact disc on in the living room, turned up the volume so she could hear it upstairs, where she looked at the children's beds, smoothed their comforters, picked up socks and underpants on Elizabeth's floor and a nightgown on Julia's, put them in the laundry basket and carried it down to the basement, emptied it into the washing machine, and poured soap on the clothes. She looked out the window at her back lawn: patches of brown grass and old snow, poplars without leaves, and pines. She breathed deeply into her stomach, exhaled singing with Ella, turned on the washing machine, took clothes from the dryer and put them in the basket, and kept singing as she climbed with the basket up the basement and second-floor stairs, and was not winded. Standing at her bed she folded the clothes, then put them in drawers in the three bedrooms. She went downstairs into the music and took out the compact disc and was in the mudroom putting on her beige parka when the phone rang. She answered the one on the kitchen wall, and Marsha said: "Do you have time for lunch after the workout?"

LuAnn heard Marsha inhaling smoke, then blowing it out.

"That sounds wonderful."

"Well, I didn't mean elegant."

"I meant your cigarette. I can have lunch."

"Don't start again. It's not as good as it sounds."

"Easy for you to say."

"If I had half your will, you'd hear me breathing air. You wouldn't even hear me. I'd be that calm."

"Half my fear. I'm going out for groceries."

"Get something sinful."

The market was in a town on the bank of the river, near its mouth at the sea. From her house she drove three miles through wooded country with widely scattered homes. She rolled down her window and let the cold air rush on her face. She did this till her gloved hands were cold and, crossing a bridge over the wide gray river, she rolled up her window, then entered a road where cars moved in single lanes and houses were built close to one another. In the hands of women and men holding steering wheels she saw cigarettes, and she imagined herself very old and strong and alert, one of those gray and wrinkled widows with wonderful eyes. She turned into the shopping center.

In the warm and brightly lit store she slowly pushed a cart. When she was single, and living and working in Boston, she went quickly through stores like this one, snatching cereal and fruit, cookies, cheeses and sliced meat; for dinners she chose food she only had to pour from a can or heat in its package, and she brought home no more than she could carry, walking to her apartment. Often she did not shop till her refrigerator and cupboards were nearly empty. Her best meals were in restaurants with dates or women friends. Then she was married, and she wanted good dinners with Ted. He liked to cook, and on weekends they idly shopped together, and choosing and handling food with him was a new happiness: a flounder lying on ice was no longer a dead fish she must cook before it spoiled; it was part of the earth she and Ted would eat. Now that she was gathering food for Julia and Elizabeth and Sam, too, she saw it in the store as something that would become her children's flesh. As a girl she had learned about the seven sacraments of the Catholic Church, all of them but one administered by a priest; the woman and man gave each other the sacrament of matrimony. Being a mother had taught her that sacraments were her work, and their number was infinite.

As she filled the cart, she looked with compassion at women, the harried ones, some with a child or two, the women who did not have housekeepers and someone to care for their children, perhaps did not have husbands or did not have good ones, who were not going to the gym for a long workout to fulfill and relax them, who had to count the dollars they were spending, whose minds had not received the gifts that she had simply been born with, as she had been born with black hair and French blood; women who as teenagers had gone into the world as bodies and faces with personalities, and so acquired boyfriends, then men, then husbands, and children; they were the women whose work was never done because they could not pay someone else to do at least part of it. No wonder one's voice rose angrily at her small girl riding in the cart, and another grabbed her son's wrist as he reached for a cereal box, and jerked him away from the shelf. The boy's face looked immune. It was not as simple as money, LuAnn knew; it was as complex as the soul. But so often the body ruled, and when it was tired, when it was overwhelmed, venom could spread through the soul. And with money, one could soothe the body, give it rest.

Work was beginning its clandestine assault on Ted's body: he worked too hard and too long. She had liked going to work, had liked being with the people there, and more than the work itself she had liked being an educated woman with a profession; but she had loved none of it, and her happiest moment of the day had been when it ended and she could leave her desk and go out into the world she had felt for eight hours was waiting for her to join it. Ted loved his work, and did it with passion, and if it were taken from him, and if he tried to live as she did, his soul would wither, or implode. If he lost her and the children, his work would not save him. Grief would kill him. She shopped now for the children's bones and teeth, muscles and eyes and skin, and for Ted's arteries; and because he would not be with them tonight, she bought steaks to cook on the grill.

She pushed her full cart to the front of the store, stood in line behind three women at the cashier, and looked out the glass front at the parking lot and the dark sky. No one spoke. She could not hear a voice in the entire store, only the young woman at the register sliding food, and the beeping sound of the computer. Then in another line a child talked and a woman answered; in the aisles behind LuAnn were the voices of children and women, and to her left, among the fruit and vegetables, a man spoke. She leaned on her cart and it moved and she stopped it. She yawned, then looked at the cigarettes stacked in narrow shelves behind the cashier, those packages so soft and light to hold in your hand, so delightful to open and smell. She looked out at the sky, and at the covers of magazines in a rack near the line. She breathed deeply, and the computer beeped, and beeped. She could be alone anywhere without being bored, except in lines of people standing or people in cars, those imposed cessations of motion that drew on her energy more than the motion itself did. She let weight go into her hands on the handle of the cart; her shoulders sagged, and she watched the woman in front of her putting groceries on the counter. Then she glimpsed motion and looked up at the window: snow was falling. The flakes were small and blown at an angle, swirling down among the cars in the parking lot. Standing in electric light, she gazed at its beauty out there under the dark sky, and felt the old and faint dread that was always part of her thrill when she saw falling snow, as though her flesh were born or conceived with its ancestors' knowledge that this windblown white silence could entrap and freeze and kill. On the counter packages slid, and the computer beeped; then it was LuAnn's turn, and as she unloaded the cart, she looked at the young blond woman wearing the store's blue apron and said: "It looks like a storm."

"They say a nor'easter."

"Really?"

"That's what they say."

She looked at the snow. She knew that her house faced northwest and the river flowed southeast, and the market was southeast of her house, and at night she could find the North Star. But how had she become a woman who rarely knew from which direction the wind blew? She said: "I didn't hear the weather report."

"Me neither." The woman was looking down at her work. "They said it in the coffee room."

In the woman's apron pocket was the shape of a cigarette pack. LuAnn said: "Do they let you smoke?"

"We have to go outside."

"I'll turn on the car radio."

The woman looked quizzically at her, and LuAnn smiled and said: "So I'll know what I'm looking at with my own eyes."

The woman smiled, and LuAnn pushed her cart through doors that opened for her, out to the sidewalk, where she looked up at the snow and it landed on her cheeks; when she lowered her face, she saw in her path two approaching young men, both with mustaches, one wearing only a red hooded sweatshirt with his jeans. He looked at her as though he were deciding whether to buy her, and she looked down and swerved the cart around them. They wore work boots. She went to the trunk of her car and put the groceries in it. She turned to push the cart back to the store, and saw the two men standing at its front, watching her. She did not move. Then they did, walking to the left, toward the parking lot. She was afraid, and angry, too, and ashamed of her fear; she pushed the cart to the sidewalk in front of the store, and did not look to her left, where the men had walked. In the car she turned on the windshield wipers and defroster, opened the window, and drove into snow, smelling it and watching it fall. When she crossed the bridge, she looked at the river and the trees on its banks, and two seagulls flying near the water, and snow angling down to the waves. She turned onto the wooded road. It was not time yet for news on the radio; she would call the school or Marsha; if this were a storm, the school would send the children home before the roads got dangerous. A green car was perhaps a quarter of a mile behind her. If the children came home early, she and Marsha could not exercise and go someplace for lunch. At her driveway she turned and climbed the curve and drove into the garage. She opened the trunk and carried two of the bags up the steps and held them with one arm while she unlocked the door and pushed it open, crossed the mudroom, and opened the kitchen door; she put the bags on the counter, went to the answering machine in the dining room, pressed its play button, and listened to Marsha's voice: "The snow is going to stop in early afternoon. There's no snow day. See you at the gym. Let's eat at the Harborside, and have a Manhattan. Remember when people had drinks at lunch?"

A Manhattan: she imagined the stemmed glass, the brown drink, the first good sip. No, not with pretty auburn-haired Marsha, not today. She would take a drag of Marsha's cigarette, to taste and feel that with the whiskey; then she would smoke one. Marsha would protest but would give it to her anyway; then she would smoke another. No, at lunch she would drink water. She put her purse on the dining room table and thought of pushing the barbell up from her chest, exhaling as blood rushed to her muscles. She went into the kitchen, to go outside for more bags of groceries, and two men stepped out of the mudroom, through the open door: the one in the red hooded sweatshirt from the parking lot was in front; behind him was the other man, in a sky blue parka. Her mouth opened, and her body seemed to jump up and back, though her feet did not leave the floor. They had followed her all this way, half an hour from the market; they were doom walking out of the snow. The man in red stopped near the refrigerator, and the one in blue stood beside him; they were close enough to hand something to, if she stepped and reached. They stood between her and the two open doors; she saw falling snow beyond their shoulders and faces, as if it were snow in someone else's life.

She was afraid to turn and run out the front door, or the door to the deck at the other side of the house, or out the back door, down the hall between the playroom and the library; she saw herself running up the hill behind the house, into the woods; running down the sloping front lawn to the road; saw herself dying in the woods and beside the road and on the carpet near the doorway. Her body would not turn its back on them; it knew that if it did, it would die. She was looking at the brown eyes of the one in red; his mustache was brown, he had not shaved today, brown hair curled out from the front of his hood, and his eyes terrified her. There was no fear in them. In their light she saw hatred and anger, and the excitement they gave this man. The other man had darker brown hair and a mustache, and also had not shaved today. Excitement was in his eyes, but not hatred and anger, and she knew he was the follower, the one who would help with and watch whatever happened. Her mouth was still open. She willed it to shape words, utter sounds that would save her. She waited for this, waited for images to form in her mind and become words. But she saw only the eyes of the man in red, and in them she saw herself stripped naked, struck with fists, choked, raped on the floor, both of them raping her; they would take away every bit of her. Now words came to her mind, but not her open mouth: *No, God; not like this.*

Fury rushed with her fear, and she trembled as her soul gathered itself into her blood and muscles. The man in red lifted a hand to his brow and pushed back his hood; his brown curls stirred, and the hood settled behind his neck. Then her left foot was striding quickly forward once, and she watched her right leg and booted foot kicking upward, felt her knee lock before her foot struck the testicles of the man in red. She was amazed; her heart was a flood that filled her chest; she watched his head and torso come forward and down, heard him gasp and groan. Her body was moving, swinging a backhanded left fist at the other man; she saw the one in red fall to his knees and saw her knuckles graze the nose of the one in blue. He pushed her across the room, her back struck the counter near the stove, and he was coming with closed fists and angry eyes. On the counter to her left she saw the teakettle, its copper surface animate, drawing her to it; with her right hand she reached across her body and gripped the handle; she spun to her right, her arm extended, and released the kettle, but his face was gone; the kettle was in the air above his lowered head, then hitting a cabinet. Within the sound of that, she was moving to her left to the skillet on the stove; she grabbed its wooden handle as the kettle hit the floor. She swung backhanded, holding the skillet flat, and its side hit his nose, above his rising hands; blood flowed and she was lifting the skillet with two hands above her head, swinging it to his fore-head and the fingers of one hand. His body lowered, his head level now with hers. She hit the top of his head twice; blood was on his mouth and chin and parka, and she felt the man in red to her right; her body was al-ready starting to move toward him as for the third time she hit the head of the man in blue, and he fell.

She leaped to her right: the man in red was on his knees, holding the counter by the refrigerator with his left hand, pulling himself up; his face was pale, and with the anger and hatred in his eyes was pain. She swung the skillet two-handed, from left to right; he lifted his right hand to his face, and with the skillet's bottom she hit his fingers and cheekbone, and knocked his head against the counter. The sound of the blow filled her; the shock of it danced in her. She swung again, hitting his hand and face; and again, smelling blood and saliva from his mouth; then she raised the skillet over her head and hit his brow, and his right hand dropped from his cheek, and his left hand slid off the counter. He was kneeling still; then his head and upper body fell forward, and on the floor his out-stretched hands cushioned his face as it hit. He lay bleeding onto the backs of his hands. She looked behind her: the one in blue was on his back now, both hands touching his bleeding nose and lips. She ran to the phone and faced them. They rolled onto their sides, their stomachs, and began pushing themselves up with their arms and legs. She raised the skillet with her right hand and held the phone in her left.

They were crawling away from her. The one in blue stood, weaved once, then bent to the man in red and held his armpits and pulled him upward. The man groaned. Blood was on the floor, and the man in blue had his arm around the waist of the one in red; they went past the refrigerator and into the mudroom. She stood holding the phone and the skillet. They went out the door and down the steps; snow landed on their shoulders and heads. She was breathing fast; the sound of it filled the room. She looked out the doors at snow and, beyond the driveway, a large pine tree. Then she dropped the phone and ran to the steps and stopped. The man in red was in the passenger seat of the car, his hands at his face; the one in blue was starting it. She stood on the top step, holding the skillet with both hands. When the man in blue backed the car and turned it to go downhill, she ran down the steps and stood on snow and read the numbers on the license plate, repeated them aloud as she ran into the mud-room, closed and locked the door, went into the kitchen, closed and locked that door, saying: "Six two seven seven three one."

She faced the door, holding the skillet in her right hand, and picked up the dangling and beeping phone, repeating the license number aloud as her finger pressed nine and one and one.

The two men vanished, and she would never see them again. They remained part of her life: their eyes looking at her before she kicked, and swung the skillet; the feel of her foot striking, and the feel and sound of the skillet hitting skin and bone; the pain in their eyes then; their blood. From the parking lot of the shopping center they had stolen the car they followed her in; they left it at a mall west of her house and stole another, which they left at a hospital in Albany, where they gave names that were probably not theirs and paid cash to have their noses set, then stole a nurse's car that Chicago police found without its tires and radio near the train station.

She told her story first to Ted on the phone, while she waited for the cruiser; then to the young officer who came with the siren on, and whom she asked for a ciga-rette. He did not smoke. The snow stopped falling while he helped her carry in the groceries. Then she told it to the tall graying detective in a tan overcoat who came to show her photographs of men who broke into houses, and to dust for fingerprints and take samples of blood. He had cigarettes and she smoked and sat at the dining room table and looked at pictures of men whom she had never seen. The detective took off his suit coat and rolled up his sleeves and filled a bucket with hot water, and they kneeled on the floor and with sponges washed the blood from the tile, standing to wring the sponges over the sink. She was doing this when Marsha called from the gym, and she told Marsha the story while the detective emptied the bucket into the sink and began washing it. He gave her a cigarette and left, and Marsha came, trotting from the car, and made tea and gave her cigarettes and LuAnn told her again. Ted phoned to tell her when his flight would arrive in Boston that night; he would be home before the children were in bed, and he was not going to work tomorrow; he was not going to work until they had an alarm system, and its remote control was in her purse.

"In case more than you can handle show up," he said. "*Twen*ty guys or so."

Marsha called her husband and told him, and said to come to LuAnn's after work; then she gave LuAnn her cigarettes and left to get her children at school and buy more steaks. At three-thirty LuAnn went outside and looked at snow on the earth and gathered on wide branches of pines. She said: "Thank You." Then she looked up at the gray sky. "That I didn't get killed. That I didn't get raped. That I didn't miss his balls. That I didn't miss with the skillet. That I didn't beg for their mercy. That I didn't kill anyone."

She lowered her face to the earth before her and

walked down the driveway and waited for the yellow bus to come around the curve of snow and green and gray trees. When it came, she crouched and hugged Julia and Elizabeth and Sam, and climbed to the house, where in the living room fireplace she stacked logs and started a fire, and they sat on cushions before it, and she told them her story. She stood and showed them how she had kicked, and how she had swung the skillet, her empty hands clenched tightly, her arms quick, and she watched her children's dark and wondering eyes, lit by fire.

Near midnight, the upstairs hall was lighted, all the downstairs rooms were dark, and in front of the burning logs she sat with Ted on cushions. She said: "When I came out of the store and the one in red looked at me the way he did, I looked down. I pushed the cart to the car and put the groceries in the trunk. I was pissed off, but that was going away. I could see the groceries, feel their weight in my hands; feel the snow on my face, and smell it. Then I turned to push the cart back, and they were still there."

She took a cigarette from the second pack Marsha had given her, and looked at Ted's eyes. "I'll quit again tomorrow. This strange sacrament from the earth."

He smiled.

"I've never told you this," she said. "But there's something about taking the cart back instead of leaving it in the parking lot. I don't know when this came to me; it was a few years ago. There's a difference between leaving it where you empty it and taking it back to the front of the store. It's significant."

"Because somebody has to take them in."

"Yes. And if you know that, and you do it for that

one guy, you do something else. You join the world. With your body. And for those few moments, you join it with your soul. You move out of your isolation and become universal. But they were standing there watching me. Then I was afraid: a woman so far removed from nature that the checkout clerk had to tell me which way the wind was blowing. And she heard it from someone in the coffee room. Then the men left, and I pushed the cart back. I live by trying to be what I'm doing. I could do nearly everything I do without thinking about it. But I'd be different."

His face was tender in the light of the fire; he said: "Yes."

"They collided with me: all this harmony I work for; this life of the spirit with the flesh. They walked into the kitchen and I said *No, God; not like this,* and I beat them with a skillet. But I'm not sure that was the answer to my prayer."

"It was."

"I don't know."

"What else could you have done?"

"I can't think of anything else. I know what I couldn't do. I couldn't turn the other cheek."

"Listen," he said, and he leaned closer and placed both palms on her cheeks. "You did what you had to do. It's a jungle out there."

"No. It's not out there. Everything is out there, and everything is in here." She touched her heart. "Hitting them, seeing their blood, seeing them fall. All afternoon I was amazed at my body. But that was me hitting them."

He lowered his hands, rested one on her shoulder,

and said: "You *had* to. For yourself. For the children. For me."

"I don't even know what they wanted."

"You saw it in their eyes."

"I know what I wanted. And, no, I don't think I have the right to give away my life. Because of you and the children. I think the one in red wanted to rape me. Maybe that was all. Then the other one probably would have, too."

"*All?* LuAnn, that's reason enough to beat them till . . ." He paused, looking at her eyes. She could see him imagining himself attacking the two men. She said: "Till they were dead? On the kitchen floor? I don't know how close I came to killing them. Who knows, when you hit someone's face and head with a steel skillet? I'd do it again. But I have to know this, and remember this, and tell it to the children: I didn't hit those men so I could be alive for the children, or for you. I hit them so my blood would stay in my body; so I could keep breathing. And if it's that easy, how are we supposed to live? If evil can walk through the door, and there's a place deep in our hearts that knows how to look at its face, and beat it till it's broken and bleeding, till it crawls away. And we do this with rapture."

He moved closer to her. Their legs touched, their hips, their arms; and they sat looking at the fire.

Dancing After Hours

FOR M.L.

EMILY MOORE WAS A FORTY-YEAR-OLD bartender in a town in Massachusetts. On a July evening, after making three margaritas and giving them to Kay to take to a table, and drawing four mugs of beer for two young couples at the bar, wearing bathing suits and sweatshirts and smelling of sunscreen, she went outside to see the sun before it set. She blinked and stood on the landing of the wooden ramp that angled down the front wall of the bar. She smelled hot asphalt; when the wind blew from the east, she could smell the ocean here, and at her apartment, and sometimes she smelled it in the rain, but now the air was still. In front of the bar was a road, and across it were white houses and beyond them was a hill with green trees. A few cars passed. She looked to her right, at a grassy hill where the road curved; above the hill, the sun was low and the sky was red.

Emily wore a dark blue shirt with short sleeves and a pale yellow skirt; she had brown hair, and for over thirty years she had wanted a pretty face. For too long, as a girl and adolescent, then a young woman, she had believed her face was homely. Now she knew it was simply not pretty. Its parts were: her eyes, her nose, her mouth, her cheeks and jaw, and chin and brow; but, combined, they lacked the mysterious proportion of a pretty face during Emily's womanhood in America. Often, looking at photographs of models and actresses, she thought how disfiguring an eighth of an inch could be, if a beautiful woman's nose were moved laterally that distance, or an eye moved vertically. Her body had vigor, and beneath its skin were firm muscles, and for decades her female friends had told Emily they envied it. They admired her hair, too: it was thick and soft and fell in waves to her shoulders.

Believing she was homely as a girl and a young woman had deeply wounded her. She knew this affected her when she was with people, and she knew she could do nothing but feel it. She could not change. She also liked her face, even loved it; she had to: it held her eyes and nose and mouth and ears; they let her see and hear and smell and taste the world; and behind her face was her brain. Alone in her apartment, looking in the mirror above her dressing table, she saw her entire life, perhaps her entire self, in her face, and she could see it as it was when she was a child, a girl, a young woman. She knew now that most people's faces were plain, that most women of forty, even if they had been lovely once, were plain. But she felt that her face was an injustice she had suffered, and no matter how hard she tried, she could not achieve some new clarity, could not see herself as an ordinary and attractive woman walking the earth within meeting radius of hundreds of men whose eyes she could draw, whose hearts she could inspire.

On the landing outside the bar, she was gazing at the trees and blue sky and setting sun, and smelling the exhaust of passing cars. A red van heading east, with a black man driving and a white man beside him, turned left from the road and came into the parking lot. Then she saw that the white man sat in a wheelchair. Emily had worked here for over seven years, had never had a customer in a wheelchair, and had never wondered why the front entrance had a ramp instead of steps. The driver parked in a row of cars facing the bar, with an open space of twenty feet or so between the van and the ramp; he reached across the man in the wheelchair and closed the window and locked the door, then got out and walked around to the passenger side. The man in the wheelchair looked to his right at Emily and smiled; then, still looking at her, he moved smoothly backward till he was at the door behind the front seat, and turned his chair to face the window. Emily returned the smile. The black man turned a key at the side of the van, there was the low sound of a motor, and the door swung open. On a lift, the man in the wheelchair came out and, smiling at her again, descended to the ground. The wheelchair had a motor, and the man moved forward onto the asphalt, and the black man turned the key, and the lift rose and went into the van and the door closed.

Emily hoped the man's injury was not to his brain as

well; she had a long shift ahead of her, until one o'clock closing, and she did not want the embarrassment of trying to speak to someone and listen to someone whose body was anchored in a chair and whose mind was afloat. She did not want to feel this way, but she knew she had no talent for it, and she would end by talking to him as though he were an infant, or a dog. He moved across the parking lot, toward the ramp and Emily. She turned to her right, so she faced him, and the sun.

The black man walked behind him but did not touch the chair. He wore jeans and a red T-shirt, he was tall and could still be in his twenties, and he exercised: she guessed with medium weights and running. The man in the moving chair wore a pale blue shirt with the cuffs rolled up twice at his wrists, tan slacks, and polished brown loafers. Emily glanced at his hands, their palms up and fingers curled and motionless on the armrests of his chair; he could work the chair's controls on the right armrest, but she knew he had not polished the loafers; knew he had not put them on his feet either, and had not put on his socks, or his pants and shirt. His clothes fit him loosely and his body looked small; *arrested*, she thought, and this made his head seem large, though it was not. She wanted to treat him well. She guessed he was in his mid-thirties, but all she saw clearly in his face was his condition: he was not new to it. His hair was brown, thinning on top, and at the sides it was combed back and trimmed. Someone took very good care of this man, and she looked beyond him at the black man's eyes. Then she pulled open the door, heard the couples in bathing suits and the couples at tables and the men at the dartboard; smells of cigarette smoke and beer and liquor came from the air-conditioned dark; she liked those smells. The man in the chair was climbing the ramp, and he said: "Thank you."

His voice was normal, and so was the cheerful light in his eyes, and she was relieved. She said: "I make the drinks, too."

"This gets better."

He smiled, and the black man said: "Our kind of place, Drew. The bartender waits outside, looking for us."

Drew was up the ramp, his feet close to Emily's legs; she stepped inside, her outstretched left arm holding the door open; the black man reached over Drew and held the door and said: "I've got it."

She lowered her arm and turned to the dark and looked at Rita, who was watching from a swivel chair at the bar. Rita Bick was thirty-seven years old, and had red hair in a ponytail, and wore a purple shirt and a black skirt; she had tended bar since late morning, grilled and fried lunches, served the happy hour customers, and now was drinking a straight-up Manhattan she had made when Emily came to work. Her boyfriend had moved out a month ago, and she was smoking again. When Emily had left the bar to see the evening sun, she had touched Rita's shoulder in passing, then stopped when Rita said quietly: "What's so great about living a long time? Remote controls?" Emily had said: "What?" and Rita had said: "To change channels. While you lie in bed alone." Emily did not have a television in her bedroom, so she would not lie in bed with a remote control, watching movies and parts of movies till near dawn, when she could finally sleep. Now Rita stood and put her cigarette between her lips and pushed a table and four chairs out of Drew's path, then another table and its chairs, and at the next table she pulled away two chairs, and Drew rolled past Emily, the black man following, the door swinging shut on the sunlight. Emily watched Drew moving to the place Rita had made. Rita took the cigarette from her lips and looked at Drew.

"Will this be all right?"

"Absolutely. I like the way you make a road."

He turned his chair to the table and stopped, his back to the room, his face to the bar. Rita looked at Emily and said: "She'll do the rest. I'm off."

"Then join us. You left two chairs."

Emily was looking at the well-shaped back of the black man when he said: "Perfect math."

"Sure," Rita said, and went to the bar for her purse and drink. Emily stepped toward the table to take their orders, but Kay was coming from the men at the dartboard with a tray of glasses and beer bottles, and she veered to the table. Emily went behind the bar, a rectangle with a wall at one end and a swinging door to the kitchen. When Jeff had taught her the work, he had said: When you're behind the bar, you're the ship's captain; never leave the bar, and never let a customer behind it; keep their respect. She did. She was friendly with her customers; she wanted them to feel they were welcome here, and were missed if they did not come in often. She remembered the names of the regulars, their jobs and something about their families, and what they liked to drink. She talked with them when they wanted her to, and this was the hardest work of all; and standing for hours was hard, and she wore runner's shoes, and still her soles ached. She did not allow discourtesy or drunkenness.

The long sides of the bar were parallel to the building's front and rear, and the couples in bathing suits faced the entrance and, still talking, glanced to their right at Drew. Emily saw Drew notice them; he winked at her, and she smiled. He held a cigarette between his curled fingers. Kay was talking to him and the black man, holding her tray with one arm. Emily put a Bill Evans cassette in the player near the cash register, then stepped to the front of the bar and watched Kay in profile: the left side of her face, her short black hair, and her small body in a blue denim skirt and a black silk shirt. She was thirty and acted in the local theater and performed on nights when Emily was working, and she was always cheerful at the bar. Emily never saw her outside the bar, or Rita, either; she could imagine Rita at home because Rita told her about it; she could only imagine about Kay that she must sometimes be angry, or sad, or languid. Kay turned from the table and came six paces to the bar and put her tray on it; her eyelids were shaded, her lipstick pale. Emily's concentration when she was working was very good: the beach couples were talking and she could hear each word and Evans playing the piano and, at the same time, looking at Kay, she heard only her, as someone focusing on one singer in a chorus hears only her, and the other singers as well.

"Two margaritas, straight up, one in a regular glass because he has trouble with stems. A Manhattan for Rita. She says it's her last."

Dark-skinned, black-haired Kay Younger had gray-blue eyes, and she flirted subtly and seriously with Rita, evening after evening when Rita sat at the bar for two drinks after work. Rita smiled at Kay's flirting, and Emily did not believe she saw what Emily did: that Kay was falling in love. Emily hoped Kay would stop the fall, or direct its arc toward a woman who did not work at the bar. Emily wished she were not so cautious, or disillusioned; she longed for love but was able to keep her longing muted till late at night when she lay reading in bed, and it was trumpets, drums, French horns; and when she woke at noon, its sound in her soul was a distant fast train. Love did not bring happiness, it did not last, and it ended in pain. She did not want to believe this, and she was not certain that she did; perhaps she feared it was true in her own life, and her fear had become a feeling that tasted like disbelief. She did not want to see Rita and Kay in pain, and she did not want to walk into their pain when five nights a week she came to work. Love also pulled you downhill; then you had to climb again to the top, where you felt solidly alone with your integrity and were able to enjoy work again, and food and exercise and friends. Kay lit a cigarette and rested it on an ashtray, and Emily picked it up and drew on it and put it back; she blew smoke into the ice chest and reached for the tequila in the speed rack.

The beach couples and dart throwers were gone, someone sat on every chair at the bar, and at twelve of the fifteen tables, and Jeff was in his place. He was the manager, and he sat on the last chair at the back of the bar, before its gate. A Chet Baker cassette was playing, and Emily was working fast and smoothly, making drinks, washing glasses, talking to customers who spoke to her, punching tabs on the cash register, putting money in it, giving change, and stuffing bills and dropping coins into the brandy snifter that held her tips. Rita took her empty glass to Emily; it had been her second Manhattan and she had sipped it, had sat with Drew and the black man while they drank three margaritas. There were no windows in the bar, and Emily imagined the quiet dusk outside and Rita in her purple shirt walking into it. She said: "Jeff could cook you a steak."

"That's sweet. I have fish at home. And a potato. And salad."

"It's good that you're cooking."

"Do you? At night."

"It took me years."

"Amazing."

"What?"

"How much will it takes. I watch TV while I eat. But I cook. If I stay and drink with these guys, it could be something I'd start doing. Night shifts are better."

"I can't sleep anyway."

"I didn't know that. You mean all the time?"

"Every night, since college."

"Can you take a pill?"

"I read. Around four I sleep."

"I'd go crazy. See you tomorrow."

"Take care."

Rita turned and waved at Drew and the black man and walked to the door, looking at no one, and went outside. Emily imagined her walking into her apartment, listening to her telephone messages, standing at the machine, her heart beating with hope and dread; then putting a potato in the oven, taking off her shoes, turning on the television, to bring light and sound, faces and bodies into the room.

Emily had discipline: every night she read two or three poems twice, then a novel or stories till she slept. Eight hours later she woke and ate grapefruit or a melon, and cereal with a banana or berries and skimmed milk, and wheat toast with nothing on it. An hour after eating, she left her apartment and walked five miles in fifty-three minutes; the first half mile was in her neighborhood, and the next two were on a road through woods and past a farm with a meadow where cows stood. In late afternoon she cooked fish or chicken, and rice, a yellow vegetable and a green one. On the days when she did not have to work, she washed her clothes and cleaned her apartment, bought food, and went to a video store to rent a movie, or in a theater that night watched one with women friends. All of this sustained her body and soul, but they also isolated her: she became what she could see and hear, smell and taste and touch; like and dislike; think about and talk about; and they became the world. Then, in her long nights, when it seemed everyone on earth was asleep while she lay reading in bed, sorrow was tangible in the dark hall to her bedroom door, and in the dark rooms she could not see from her bed. It was there, in the lamplight, that she knew she would never bear and love children; that tomorrow would require of her the same strength and rituals of today; that if she did not nourish herself with food, gain a balancing peace of soul with a long walk, and immerse herself in work, she could not keep sorrow at bay, and it would consume her. In the lamplight she read, and she was opened to the world by imagined women and men and children, on pages she held in her hands, and the sorrow in the darkness remained, but she was consoled, as she became one with the earth and its creatures: its dead, its living, its living after her own death; one with the sky and water, and with a single leaf falling from a tree.

A man at the bar pushed his empty glass and beer bottle toward Emily, and she opened a bottle and brought it with a glass. Kay was at her station with a tray of glasses, and said: "Rita left."

"Being brave."

Emily took a glass from the tray and emptied it in one of two cylinders in front of her; a strainer at its top caught the ice and fruit; in the second cylinder she dipped the glass in water, then placed it in the rack of the small dishwasher. She looked at each glass she rinsed and at all three sides of the bar as she listened to Kay's order. Then she made piña coladas in the blender, whose noise rose above the music and the voices at the bar, and she made gin and tonics, smelling the wedges of lime she squeezed; and made two red sea breezes. Kay left with the drinks and Emily stood facing the tables, where the room was darker, and listened to Baker's trumpet. She tapped her fingers in rhythm on the bar. Behind her was Jeff, and she felt him watching her.

Jefferson Gately was a tall and broad man who had lost every hair on top of his head; he had brown hair on the sides and back, and let it grow over his collar. He had a thick brown mustache with gray in it. Last fall, when the second of his two daughters started college, his wife told him she wanted a divorce. He was shocked. He was an intelligent and watchful man, and at work he was gentle, and Emily could not imagine him living twenty-three years with a woman and not knowing precisely when she no longer wanted him in her life. He told all of this to Emily on autumn nights, with a drink after the bar closed, and she believed he did not know his wife's heart, but she did not understand why. He lived alone in a small apartment, and his brown eyes were often pensive. At night he sat on his chair and watched the crowd and drank club soda with bitters; when people wanted food, he cooked hamburgers or steaks on the grill, potatoes and clams or fish in the fryers, and made sandwiches and salads. The bar's owner was old and lived in Florida and had no children, and Jeff would inherit the bar. Twice a year he flew to Florida to eat dinner with the old man, who gave Jeff all his trust and small yearly pay raises.

In spring Jeff had begun talking differently to Emily, when she was not making drinks, when she went to him at the back of the bar. He still talked only about his daughters and the bar, or wanting to buy a boat to ride in on the river, to fish from on the sea; but he sounded as if he were confiding in her; and his eyes were giving her something: they seemed poised to reveal a depth she could enter if she chose. One night in June he asked Emily if she would like to get together sometime, maybe for lunch. The muscles in her back and chest and legs and arms tightened, and she said: "Why not," and saw in his face that her eyes and voice had told him no and that she had hurt him.

She had hurt herself, too, and she could not say this to Jeff: she wanted to have lunch with him. She liked him, and lunch was in daylight and not dangerous; you met at the restaurant and talked and ate, then went home, or shopping for groceries or beach sandals. She wanted to have drinks and dinner with him, too, but dinner was timeless; there could be coffee and brandy, and it was night and you parted to sleep; a Friday dinner could end Saturday morning, in a shower that soothed your skin but not your heart, which had opened you to pain. Now there was AIDS, and she did not want to risk death for something that was already a risk, something her soul was too tired to grapple with again. She did not keep condoms in her apartment because two winters ago, after one night with a thin, pink-faced, sweet-eyed man who never called her again, she decided that next time she made love she would know about it long before it happened, and she did not need to be prepared for sudden passion. She put her box of condoms in a grocery bag and then in a garbage bag, and on a cold night after work she put the bag on the sidewalk in front of her apartment. In a drawer, underneath her stacked underwear, she had a vibrator. On days when most of her underwear was in the laundry basket, the vibrator moved when she opened and closed the drawer, and the sound of fluted plastic rolling on wood made her feel caught by someone who watched, someone who was above this. She loved what the vibrator did, and was able to forget it was there until she wanted it, but once in a while she felt shame, thinking of dying, and her sister or brother or parents finding the vibrator. Sometimes after using it, she wept.

It was ten-fifteen by the bar clock that Jeff kept twenty minutes fast. Tonight he wore a dark brown shirt with short sleeves, and white slacks; his arms and face and the top of his head were brown, with a red hue from the sun, and he looked clean and confident. It was a weekday, and in the afternoon he had fished from a party boat. He had told Emily in winter that his rent for a bedroom, a living room, a kitchen, and bathroom was six hundred dollars a month; his car was old; and until his wife paid him half the value of the house she had told him to leave, he could not buy a boat. He paid fifteen dollars to go on the party boat and fish for half a day, and when he did this, he was visibly happier. Now Emily looked at him, saw his glass with only ice in it, and brought him a club soda with a few drops of bitters; the drink was the color of Kay's lipstick. He said: "I'm going to put wider doors on the bathroom." Their faces were close over the bar, so the woman sitting to the right of Jeff could not hear unless she eavesdropped. "That guy can't get in."

"I think he has a catheter. His friend took something to the bathroom."

"I know. But the next one in a chair may want to use a toilet. He likes Kay. He can feel everything, but only in his brain and heart."

She had seen Drew talking to Kay and smiling at her, and now she realized that she had seen him as a man living outside of passion. She looked at Jeff's eyes, feeling that her soul had atrophied; that it had happened without her notice. Jeff said: "What?"

"I should have known."

"No. I had a friend like him. He always looked happy and I knew he was never happy. A mine got him, in Vietnam."

"Were you there?"

"Not with him. I knew him before and after."

"But you were there."

"Yes."

She saw herself facedown in a foxhole while the earth exploded as close to her as the walls of the bar. She said: "I couldn't do that."

"Neither could I."

"Now, you mean."

"Now, or then."

"But you did."

"I was lucky. We used to take my friend fishing. His chair weighed two hundred and fifty pounds. We carried him up the steps and lifted him over the side. We'd bait for him, and he'd fold his arms around the rod. When he got a bite, we'd reel it in. Mike looked happy on a boat. But he got very tired."

"Where is he now?"

"He died."

"Is he the reason we have a ramp?"

"Yes. But he died before I worked here. One winter pneumonia killed him. I just never got to the bathroom doors."

"You got a lot of sun today."

"Bluefish, too."

"Really?"

"You like them?"

"On the grill. With mayonnaise and lemon."

"In foil. I have a grill on my deck. It's not really a deck. It's a landing outside the kitchen, on the second floor. The size of a closet."

"There's Kay. I hope you had sunscreen."

He smiled and shook his head, and she went to Kay,

thinking they were like that: they drank too much; they got themselves injured; they let the sun burn their skin; they went to war. The cautious ones bored her. Kay put down her tray of glasses and slid two filled ashtrays to Emily, who emptied them in the garbage can. Kay wiped them with a paper napkin and said: "Alvin and Drew want steak and fries. No salads. Margaritas now, and Tecates with the meal."

"Alvin."

"Personal care attendant. His job."

"They look like friends."

"They are."

Emily looked at Jeff, but he had heard and was standing; he stepped inside the bar and went through the swinging door to the kitchen. Emily rubbed lime on the rims of glasses and pushed them into the container of thick salt, scooped ice into the blender and poured tequila, and imagined Alvin cutting Drew's steak, sticking the fork into a piece, maybe feeding it to him; and that is when she knew that Alvin wiped Drew's shit. Probably as Drew lay on his bed, Alvin lifted him and slid a bedpan under him; then he would have to roll him on one side to wipe him clean, and take the bedpan to the toilet. Her body did not shudder, but she felt as if it shuddered; she knew her face was composed, but it seemed to grimace. She heard Roland Kirk playing tenor saxophone on her cassette, and words at the bar, and voices from the tables; she breathed the smells of tequila and cigarette smoke, gave Kay the drinks, then looked at Alvin. Kay went to the table and bent forward to place the drinks. Drew spoke to her. Alvin bathed him somehow, too, kept his flesh clean for his morale and health. She looked at Alvin for too long; he turned and looked at her. She looked away, at the front door.

It was not the shit. Shit was nothing. It was the spiritual pain that twisted her soul: Drew's helplessness, and Alvin reaching into it with his hands. She had stopped teaching because of pain: she had gone with passion to high school students, year after year, and always there was one student, or even five, who wanted to feel a poem or story or novel, and see more clearly because of it. But Emily's passion dissolved in the other students. They were young and robust, and although she knew their apathy was above all a sign of their being confined by classrooms and adolescence, it still felt like apathy. It made Emily feel isolated and futile, and she thought that if she were a gym teacher or a teacher of dance, she could connect with her students. The women and men who coached athletic teams or taught physical education or dance seemed always to be in harmony with themselves and their students. In her last three years she realized she was becoming scornful and bitter, and she worked to control the tone of her voice, and what she said to students, and what she wrote on their papers. She taught without confidence or hope, and felt like a woman standing at a roadside, reading poems aloud into the wind as cars filled with teenagers went speeding by. She was tending bar in summer and finally she asked Jeff if she could work all year. She liked the work, she stopped taking sleeping pills because when she slept no longer mattered, and, with her tips, she earned more money. She did not want to teach again, or work with teenagers, or have to talk to anyone about the books she read. But she knew that pain had defeated her, while other teachers had endured it, or had not felt it as sharply.

Because of pain, she had turned away from Jeff, a man whom she looked forward to seeing at work. She was not afraid of pain; she was tired of it; and sometimes she thought being tired of it was worse than fear, that losing fear meant she had lost hope as well. If this were true, she would not be able to love with her whole heart, for she would not have a whole heart; and only a man who had also lost hope, and who would settle for the crumbs of the feast, would return her love with the crumbs of his soul. For a long time she had not trusted what she felt for a man, and for an even longer time, beginning in high school, she had deeply mistrusted what men felt for her, or believed they felt, or told her they felt. She chronically believed that, for a man, love was a complicated pursuit of an orgasm, and its evanescence was directly proportionate to the number of orgasms a particular man achieved, before his brain cleared and his heart cooled. She suspected this was also true of herself, though far less often than it was for a man.

When a man's love for Emily ended, she began to believe that he had never loved her; that she was a homely fool, a hole where the man had emptied himself. She would believe this until time healed the pain. Then she would know that in some way the man had loved her. She never believed her face was what first attracted these men; probably her body had, or something she said; but finally they did like her face; they looked at it, touched it with their hands, kissed it. She only knew now, as a forty-year-old woman who had never lived with a man, that she did not know the truth: if sexual organs were entities that drew people along with them, forcing them to collide and struggle, she wanted to be able to celebrate them; if the heart with intrepid fervor could love again and again, using the sexual organs in its dance, she wanted to be able to exalt its resilience. But nothing was clear, and she felt that if she had been born pretty, something would be clear, whether or not it were true.

She wanted equilibrium: she wanted to carry what she had to carry, and to walk with order and strength. She had never been helpless, and she thought of Drew: his throbless penis with a catheter in it, his shit. If he could not feel a woman, did he even know if he was shitting? She believed she could not bear such helplessness, and would prefer death. She thought: *I can walk. Feed myself. Shower. Shit in a toilet. Make love.* She was neither grateful nor relieved; she was afraid. She had never imagined herself being crippled, and now, standing behind the bar, she felt her spine as part of her that could be broken, the spinal cord severed; saw herself in a wheelchair with a motor, her body attenuating, her face seeming larger; saw a hired woman doing everything for her and to her.

Kay's lighter and cigarettes were on the bar; Emily lit one, drew on it twice, and placed it on the ashtray. Kay was coming out of the dark of the tables, into the dim light at the bar. She picked up the cigarette and said: "Oh, look. It came lit."

She ordered, and Emily worked with ice and limes and vodka and gin and grapefruit juice and salt, with club soda and quinine water, and scotch and bottles of beer and clean glasses, listening to Roland Kirk and remembering him twenty years ago in the small club on the highway, where she sat with two girlfriends. The place was dark, the tables so close to each other that the waitresses sidled, and everyone sat facing the bandstand and the blind black man wearing sunglasses. He had a rhythm section and a percussionist, and sometimes he played two saxophones at once. He grinned; he talked to the crowd, his head moving as if he were looking at them. He said: "It's nice, coming to work blind. Not seeing who's fat or skinny. Ugly. Or pretty. Know what I mean?"

Emily knew then, sitting between her friends, and knew now, working in this bar that was nearly as dark as the one where he had played; he was dead, but here he was, his music coming from the two speakers high on the walls, coming softly. Maybe she was the only person in the bar who heard him at this moment, as she poured gin; of course everyone could hear him, as people heard rain outside their walls. In the bar she never heard rain or cars, or saw snow or dark skies or sunlight. Maybe Jeff was listening to Kirk while he cooked. And only to be kind, to immerse herself in a few seconds of pure tenderness, she took two pilsner glasses from the shelf and opened the ice chest and pushed the glasses deep into the ice, for Alvin and Drew.

Kirk had walked the earth with people who only saw. So did Emily. But she saw who was fat or ugly, and if they were men, she saw them as if through an upstairs window. Twenty years ago, Kirk's percussionist stood beside him, playing a tambourine, and Kirk was improvising, playing fast, and Emily was drumming with her hands on the table. Kirk reached to the percussionist and touched his arm and stepped toward the edge of the bandstand. The percussionist stepped off it and held up his hand; Kirk took it and stepped down and followed the percussionist, followed the sound of the tambourine, playing the saxophone, his body swaying. People stood and pushed their tables and chairs aside, and, clapping and exclaiming, followed Kirk. Everyone was standing, and often Kirk reached out and held someone's waist, and hugged. In the dark they came toward Emily, who was standing with her friends. The percussionist's hand was fast on his tambourine; he was smiling; he was close; then he passed her, and Kirk was there. His left arm encircled her, his hand pressing her waist; she smelled his sweat as he embraced her so hard that she lost balance and stood on her toes; she could feel the sound of the saxophone in her body. He released her. People were shouting and clapping, and she stepped into the line, held the waist of a man in front of her; her two friends were behind her, one holding her waist. She was making sounds but not words, singing with Kirk's saxophone. They weaved around tables and chairs, then back to the bandstand, to the drummer and the bass and piano players, and the percussionist stepped up on it and turned to Kirk, and Kirk took his hand and stepped up and faced the clapping, shouting crowd. Then Kirk, bending back, blew one long high note, then lowered his head and played softly, slowly, some old and sweet melody. Emily's hands, raised and parted to clap, lowered to her sides. She walked backward to her table, watching Kirk. She and her friends quietly pulled their table and chairs into place and sat. Emily quietly sat, and waitresses moved in the dark, bent close to the mouths of people softly ordering drinks. The music was soothing, was loving, and Emily watched Kirk and felt that everything good was possible.

It would be something like that, she thought now, *something ineffable that comes from outside and fills us; something that changes the way we see what we see; something that allows us to see what we don't.*

She served four people at the bar, and Jeff came through the swinging door with two plates and forks and knives, and went through the gate and around the bar to Alvin and Drew. He stood talking to them; Alvin took the plate Jeff had put in front of Drew, and began cutting the steak. Jeff walked back to the bar, and Emily opened two bottles of Tecate and pulled the glasses out of the ice chest. Jeff said: "Nice, Emily."

Something lovely spread in her heart, blood warmed her cheeks, and tears were in her eyes; then they flowed down her face, stopped near her nose, and with the fingers of one hand she wiped them, and blinked and wiped her eyes, and they were clear. She glanced around the bar; no one had seen. Jeff said: "Are you all right?"

"I just had a beautiful memory of Roland Kirk."

"Lucky man." He held the bottle necks with one hand, and she put the glasses in his other hand; he held only their bottoms, to save the frost.

"I didn't know him. I saw him play once. That's him now."

"That's him? I was listening in the kitchen. The oil bubbled in time."

"My blood did, that night."

"So you cry at what's beautiful?"

"Sometimes. How about you?"

"It stays inside. I end up crying at silly movies."

He took the beer to Alvin and Drew, and stood talking; then he sat with them. A woman behind Emily at the bar called her name, and the front door opened and Rita in a peach shirt and jeans came in, and looked at Drew and Alvin and Jeff. Then she looked at Emily and smiled and came toward the bar. Emily smiled, then turned to the woman who had called; she sat with two other women. Emily said: "All around?"

"All around," the woman said.

Emily made daiquiris in the blender and brought them with both hands gripping the three stems, then went to Rita, who was standing between two men sitting at the bar. Rita said: "Home sucked." She gave Emily a five-dollar bill. "Dry vermouth on the rocks, with a twist."

Emily looked at Jeff and Alvin and Drew; they were watching and smiling. She poured Rita's drink and gave it to her and put her change on the bar, and said: "It's a glorious race."

"People?" Rita said, and pushed a dollar toward Emily. "Tell me about it."

"So much suffering, and we keep getting out of bed in the morning."

She saw the man beside Rita smiling. Emily said to him: "Don't we."

"For some reason."

"We get hungry," Rita said. "We have to pee."

She picked up the vermouth and went to Jeff and Alvin and Drew; Jeff stood and got a chair from another table. Alvin stuck Drew's fork into a piece of meat and placed the fork between Drew's fingers, and Drew raised it to his mouth. He could grip the French fries with his fingers, lift them from the plate. Kay went to their table and, holding her tray of glasses against her hip, leaned close to Rita and spoke, and Rita laughed. Kay walked smiling to the bar.

When Alvin and Drew finished eating, Drew held a cigarette and Rita gave him a light. Emily had seen him using his lighter while Rita was at home. He could not quite put out his cigarettes; he jabbed them at the ashtray and dropped them and they smoldered. Sometimes Alvin put them out, and sometimes he did not, and Emily thought about fire, where Drew lived, then wondered if he were ever alone. Jeff stood with their empty plates and went to the kitchen, and she thought of Drew, after this happened to him, learning each movement he could perform alone, and each one he could not; learning what someone else had to help him do, and what someone else had to do for him. He would have learned what different people did not like to do. Alvin did not smoke, or he had not tonight. Maybe he disliked touching cigarettes and disliked smelling them burning to the filter in an ashtray, so sometimes he put them out and sometimes smelled them. But he could empty bags of piss, and wipe shit. Probably he inserted the catheter.

Two summers ago a young woman came to work as a bartender, to learn the job while doing it. Jeff worked with her, and on her first three days the noon crowd wanted fried clams, and she told Jeff she could not stand clams but she would do it. She picked them up raw and put them in batter and fried them, and they nauseated her. She did not vomit, but she looked all through lunch as if she would. On the fourth day, Jeff cooked, but when she smelled the frying clams while she was making drinks, she could see them raw and feel them in her hands and smell them, and she was sick as she worked and talked with customers. She had learned the essential drinks in four days and most of the rare ones, and Jeff called a friend who managed a bar whose only food was peanuts, to make the customers thirsty, and got her a job.

So, was anyone boundless? Most of the time, you could avoid what disgusted you. But if you always needed someone to help you simply live, and that person was disgusted by your cigarettes, or your body, or what came out of it, you would sense that disgust, be infected by it, and become disgusted by yourself. Emily did not mind the smell of her own shit, the sight of it on toilet paper and in the water. There was only a stench if someone else smelled it, only disgust if someone else saw it. Drew's body had knocked down the walls and door of his bathroom; living without this privacy, he also had to rely on someone who did not need him to be private. It was an intimacy babies had, and people like Drew, and the ill and dying. And who could go calmly and tenderly and stoutly into his life? For years she had heard married women speak with repugnance of their husbands: their breath, their farts, their fat stomachs and asses, their lust, their golf, their humor, their passions, their loves. Maybe Jeff's wife was one of these; maybe she had been with him too long; maybe he took home too many fish.

Kirk had said: "Know what I mean?" To love without the limits of seeing; so to love without the limits of the flesh. As Kirk danced through the crowd, he had hugged women and men, not knowing till his hand and arm touched their flesh. When he hugged Emily, she had not felt like a woman in the embrace of a man; she melded; she was music.

Alvin stood and came to the bar and leaned toward her and said: "Are we close to a motel?"

"Sure. Where did you come from?"

"Boston."

"Short trip."

"First leg of one. He likes to get out and look around." He smiled. "We stopped for a beer."

"I'm glad you did. You can use the bar phone."

She picked up the telephone and the book beside the cash register and put them on the bar. She opened the Yellow Pages. Alvin said: "We need the newest one."

"Are the old ones bad?"

"Eye of a needle."

"Are you with him all the time?"

"Five days a week. Another guy takes five nights. Another the weekend, day and night. I travel with him."

"Have you always done this work?"

"No. I fell into it."

"How?"

"I wanted to do grand things. I read his ad, and called him."

"What grand things?"

"For the world. It was an abstraction."

———

Now the bar was closed and they had drawn two tables together; Emily was drinking vodka and tonic, Louis Armstrong was playing, and she listened to his trumpet, and to Drew; he was looking at her, his face passionate, joyful.

"You could do it," he said. "It's up in Maine. They teach you for—what?" He looked at Alvin. "An hour?"

"At most."

Kay said to Alvin: "Did you do it?"

"No. I don't believe in jumping out of airplanes. I don't feel good about staying inside of one, either."

"Neither do I," Emily said.

"You could do it," Drew said, watching Emily. He was drinking beer, but slowly, and he did not seem drunk. Alvin had been drinking club soda since they ate dinner. "You could come with me. They talk to you; then they take you up." Emily saw Drew being carried by Alvin and other men into a small airplane, lowered into a seat, and strapped to it. "They told me there was a ground wind. They said if I was a normal, the wind wouldn't be a problem. But—"

Jeff said: "They said 'a normal'?"

"No. What the guy said was: 'With your condition you've got a ninety percent chance of getting hurt.'" Drew smiled. "I told him I've lived with nine-to-one odds for a long time. So we went up in their little plane." Emily could not imagine being paralyzed, but she felt enclosed in a small plane; from inside the plane she saw it take off. "The guy was strong, very confident. Up in the air he lifted me out of the seat and strapped me to him. My back to his chest. We went to the door of the plane, and I looked at the blue sky."

"Weren't you terrified?" Emily lit one of Drew's cigarettes and placed it between his fingers. When she had cleaned the bar and joined them at the table, she had told him and Alvin her name. Drew Purdy. Alvin Parker. She shook their hands, Alvin rising from his chair; when Drew moved his hand upward, she had inserted hers between his fingers and his palm. His hand was soft.

"It felt like fear," Drew said. "But it was adrenaline. I didn't have any bad pictures in my head: like the chute not opening. Leaving a mess on the ground for Alvin to pray over. Then he jumped; we jumped. And I had this rush, like nothing I had ever felt. Better than anything I ever felt. And I used to do a lot, before I got hurt. But this was another world, another body. We were free-falling. Dropping down from the sky like a hawk, and everything was beautiful, green and blue. Then he opened the chute. And you know what? It was absolutely quiet up there. I was looking down at the people on the ground. They were small, and I could hear their voices. I thought I heard Alvin. Probably I imagined that. I couldn't hear words, but I could hear men and women and children. All those voices up in the sky."

Emily could see it, hear it, and her arms and breast wanted to hug him because he had done this; her hand touched his, rested on his fingers; then she took his cigarette and drew on it and put it between his fingers and blew smoke over his head.

Kay said: "I think I'd like the parachute. But I couldn't jump out of the plane."

Drew smiled. "Neither could I."

"I don't like underwater," Rita said. "And I don't like in the air."

"Tell them what happened," Alvin said.

"He didn't think I should do it."

"I thought you should do it on a different day, after what he told you. I thought you could wait."

"You knew I couldn't wait."

"Yes." Alvin looked at Emily. "It's true. He couldn't."

"I broke both my legs."

"*No*," Emily said.

Jeff said: "Did you feel them?"

Rita was shaking her head; Kay was watching Drew.

"No," Drew said. "They made a video of it. You can hear my legs break. The wind dragged us, and I couldn't do anything with my legs."

"He was laughing the whole time," Alvin said. "While the chute was pulling them on the ground. He's on top of the guy, and he's laughing and shouting: 'This is great, this is great.' And on the video you can hear his bones snapping."

"When did you know?" Jeff said.

"On the third day. When my feet were swollen, and Alvin couldn't get my shoes on."

"You never felt pain?" Rita said.

"Not like you do. It was like a pinball machine, this little ball moving around. So in the hospital they sent me a shrink. To see if I had a death wish. If a normal sky dives and breaks some bones, they don't ask him if he wanted to die. They ask quads. I told him if I wanted to die, I wouldn't have paid a guy with a parachute. I told him it was better than sex. I told him he should try it."

"What did he say?" Jeff said.

"He said he didn't think I had a death wish."

Rita said: "How did you get hurt?"

"Diving into a wave."

"Oh my God," Emily said. "I love diving into waves."

"Don't stop." He smiled. "You could slip in the shower. I know a guy like me, who fell off his bed. He wasn't drunk; he was asleep. He doesn't know how he fell. He woke up on the floor, a quad."

She was sipping her third drink and smoking one of Rita's cigarettes, and looking over Jeff's head at the wall and ceiling, listening to Paul Desmond playing saxophone with Brubeck. Rita's face was turned to Kay, and Emily could only hear their voices; Jeff and Alvin and Drew were planning to fish. She looked at them and said: "Paul Desmond—the guy playing sax—once lost a woman he loved to an older and wealthy man. One night he was sitting in a restaurant, and they came in, the young woman and the man. Desmond watched them going to their table and said: 'So this is how the world ends, not with a whim but a banker.'"

Rita and Kay were looking at her.

"I like that," Drew said.

"He was playing with a T. S. Eliot line. The poet. Who said 'April is the cruelest month.' That's why they called him T.S."

They were smiling at her. Jeff's eyes were bright.

"I used to talk this way. Five days a week."

"What were you?" Drew said.

"A teacher."

She was looking at Drew and seeing him younger, with strong arms and legs, in a bathing suit, running barefoot across hot sand to the water, his feet for the last time holding his weight on the earth, his legs moving as if they always would, his arms swinging at his sides; then he was in the surf, running still, but very slowly in the water; the cold water thrilled him, cleared his mind; he moved toward the high waves; he was grinning. Waves broke in front of him and rushed against his waist, his thighs, his penis. A rising wave crested and he dived into it as it broke, and it slapped his legs and back and turned him, turned him just so, and pushed him against the bottom.

Alvin asked Rita to dance, and Kay asked Jeff. They pushed tables and chairs and made a space on the floor, and held each other, moving to Desmond's slow song. Emily said: "When this happened to you, who pulled you out of the water?"

"Two buddies. They rode in on the wave that got me. They looked around and saw me. I was like a big rag doll in the water. I'd go under, I'd come up. Mostly under."

"Did you know how bad it was?"

"I was drowning. That's what I was afraid of till they came and got me. Then I was scared because I couldn't move. They put me on the beach, and then I felt the pain; and I couldn't move my legs and arms. I was twenty-one years old, and I knew."

Last night Emily had not worked and yesterday afternoon she had gone to the beach with a book of stories by Edna O'Brien. She rubbed sunscreen on her body and lay on a towel and read five stories. When she finished a story, she ran in the surf, and dived into a wave, opened her eyes to the salt water, stood and shook her hair and faced the beach, looking over her shoulder at the next wave coming in, then dived with it as it broke, and it pushed and pulled her to the beach, until her outstretched hands and then her face and breasts were on sand, and the surf washed over her.

John Coltrane was playing a ballad, and Jeff looked at her and said: "Would you like to dance?"

She nodded and stood, walked around tables, and in the open space turned to face him. Rita and Alvin came and started to dance. Emily took Jeff's hand and held him behind his waist, and they danced to the saxophone, her breasts touching his chest; he smelled of scotch and smoke; his mustache was soft on her brow. She looked to her left at Drew: he had turned the chair around, and was watching. Now Kay rose from her chair and stood in front of him; she bent forward, held his hands, and began to dance. She swayed to the saxophone's melody, and her feet moved in rhythm, forward, back, to her sides. Emily could not see Drew's face. She said: "I don't know if Kay should be doing that."

"He jumped from an airplane."

"But he could feel it. The thrill anyway. The air on his face."

"He can feel Kay, too. She's there. She's dancing with him." He led Emily in graceful turns toward the front wall, so she could see Drew's face. "Look. He's happy."

Drew was smiling; his head was dancing: down, up

to his right, down, up to his left. Emily looked at Jeff's eyes and said: "You told me your friend always looked happy and you knew he was never happy."

"It's complicated. I knew he couldn't *enjoy* being a quad. I knew he missed his body: fishing, hunting, swimming, dancing, girls, just *walk*ing. He probably even missed being a soldier, when he was scared and tired, and wet and hot and thirsty and bug-bit; but he was whole and strong. So I say he was never happy; he only looked happy. But he had friends, and he had fun. It took a lot of will for him to have fun. He had to do it in spite of everything. Not because of everything."

He turned her and dipped—she was leaning backward and only his arms kept her balanced; he pulled her up and held her close.

"On a fishing boat I lose myself. I don't worry about things. I just look at the ocean and feel the sun. It's the ocean. The ocean takes me there. Mike had to do it himself. He couldn't just step onto a boat and let the ocean take him. First he had to be carried on. Anybody who's helpless is afraid; you could see it in his eyes, while he joked with us. I'm sure he was sad, too, while we carried him. He was a soldier, Emily. That's not something he could forget. Then out on the ocean, he couldn't really hold the rod and fish. And his body was always pulling on him. He had spasms on the boat, and fatigue."

Coltrane softly blew a low note and held it, the drummer tapping cymbals, and the cassette ended. Emily withdrew her hand from Jeff's back, but he still held hers, and her right hand. He said: "He told me once: 'I wake up tired.' His body was his enemy, and

when he fought it, he lost. What he had to do was ignore it. That was the will. That was how he was
happy."

"Ignore it?"

"Move beyond it."

He released her back and lowered her hand, and
shifted his grip on it and held it as they walked toward
the table; then Jeff stopped her. He said: "He had
something else. He was grateful."

"For what?"

"That he wasn't blown to pieces. And that he still
had his brain."

They walked and at the table he let go of her hand
and she stood in front of Drew, and said: "You looked
good."

Kay sat beside Rita; Jeff and Alvin stood talking.

"My wife and I danced like that."

"Your wife? You said—" Then she stopped; a
woman had loved him, had married him after the wave
crippled him. She glanced past him; no one had heard.

"Right," he said. "I met her when I was like this."

"Shit."

He nodded. She said: "Would you like a beer?"

"Yes."

She walked past the table, then stopped and looked
back. Drew was turning his chair around, looking at
her now, and he said: "Do you have Old Blue Eyes?"

"Not him," Rita said.

"He's good to dance to," Kay said.

"I've got him," Emily said. "Anybody want drinks?"

She went behind the bar and made herself a vodka
and tonic. Kay and Rita came to the bar, stood with

their shoulders and arms touching, and Emily gave them a Tecate and a club soda, and they took them to Drew and Alvin. They came back and Emily put in the Sinatra cassette and poured vermouth for Rita and made a salty dog with tequila for Kay. While she was pouring the grapefruit juice, Kay said to Rita: "Can you jitterbug?"

"Girl, if you lead, I can follow."

Kay put her right hand on Rita's waist, held Rita's right hand with her left, then lifted their hands and turned Rita in a circle, letting Rita's hand turn in hers; then, facing each other, they danced. Kay sang with Sinatra:

> *Till the tune ends*
> *We're dancing in the dark*
> *And it soon ends*

Emily sang:

> *We're waltzing in the wonder*
> *Of why we're here*
> *Time hurries by, we're here*
> *And gone—*

Emily watched her pretty friends dancing, and looked beyond them at Jeff and Alvin, tapping the table with their fingers, watching, grinning; Drew was singing. She smiled and sang and played drums on the bar till the song ended. Then she poured Jeff a scotch on ice and went to the table with it, and he stood and pulled out the chair beside him, and she sat in it.

She looked at Drew. She could not see pallor in the bar light, but she knew from his eyes that he was very tired. Or maybe it was not his eyes; maybe she saw his fatigue because she could see Jeff's friend, tired on the fishing boat, talking and laughing with Jeff, a fishing rod held in his arms. Rita and Kay sat across from her, beside Alvin. Emily leaned in front of Jeff and said to Drew: "How are you?"

"Fine."

Her right knee was touching Jeff's thigh, her right arm resting on his, and her elbow touched his chest. For a moment she did not notice this; then she did; she was touching him as easily as she had while dancing, and holding his hand coming back to the table. She said to Drew: "You can sleep late tomorrow."

"I will. Then we'll go to Maine."

"You're *jump*ing again?"

"Not this time. We're going to look at the coast. Then we'll come back here and fish with Jeff."

She looked at Jeff, so close that her hair had touched his face as she turned. She drew back, looking at his eyes, seeing him again carrying a two-hundred-and-fifty-pound wheelchair with a man in it up the steps to the wharf, and up the steps to the boat: Jeff and Alvin and someone else, as many men as the width of the steps would allow; then on the boat at sea, Jeff standing beside Drew, helping him fish. She said: "Really? When?"

"Monday," Jeff said.

She sat erectly again and drank and glanced at Kay and Rita in profile, talking softly, smiling, their hands on the table, holding cigarettes and drinks.

———

Sinatra was singing "Angel Eyes," and Kay and Rita were dancing slowly, and Jeff and Alvin were in the kitchen making ham and cheese sandwiches. Kay was leading, holding Rita's hand between their shoulders, her right hand low on Rita's back; they turned and Emily looked at Rita's face: her eyes were closed. Her hand was lightly moving up and down Kay's back, and Emily knew what Rita was feeling: a softening thrill in her heart, a softening peace in her muscles; and Kay, too. She looked at Drew.

"You danced with your wife, you—" She stopped.

"Are you asking how we made love?"

"No. Yes."

"I can have an erection. I don't feel it. But you know what people can do in bed, if they want to."

Looking at his eyes, she saw herself with the vibrator.

"I was really asking you what happened. I just didn't have the guts."

"I met her at a party. We got married; we had a house. For three years. One guy in a *hun*dred with my kind of injury can get his wife pregnant. Then, wow, she was. Then on New Year's Eve my wife and my ex-best friend came to the bedroom, and stood there looking down at me. I'd thought they spent a lot of time in the living room, watching videos. But I never suspected till they came to the bed that night. Then I knew; just a few seconds before she told me the baby was his, I knew. You know what would have been different? If I could have packed my things and walked out of the house. It would have hurt; it would have broken my heart; but it would have been different. On the day of my divorce it was summer, and it was raining. I couldn't get into the courthouse; I couldn't go up the steps. A guy was working a jackhammer on the sidewalk, about thirty yards away. The judge came down the steps in his robe, and we're all on the sidewalk, my wife, the lawyers. My lawyer's holding an umbrella over me. The jackhammer's going and I can't hear and I'm saying: 'What? What did he say?' Then I was divorced. I looked up at my wife, and asked her if she'd like Chinese lunch and a movie."

"*Why?*"

"I couldn't let go."

She reached and held his hand.

"Oh, Drew."

She did not know what time it was, and she did not look at the clock over the bar. There was no music. She sat beside Jeff. Drew had his sandwich in both hands; he bit it, then lowered it to the plate. Alvin was chewing; he looked at Drew; then as simply as if Drew's face were his own, he reached with a paper napkin and wiped mustard from Drew's chin. Drew glanced at him, and nodded. *That's how he says thank you,* Emily thought. One of a hundred ways he would have learned. She picked up her sandwich, looked across the table at Kay and Rita chewing small bites, looked to her right at Jeff's cheek bulging as he chewed. She ate, and drank. Kay said: "Let's go to my house, and dance all night."

"What about your neighbors?" Rita said.

"I don't have neighbors. I have a house."

"A whole house?"

"Roof. Walls. Lawn and trees."

"I haven't lived in a house since I grew up," Rita said.

"I've got to sleep," Drew said.

Alvin nodded.

"Me, too," Jeff said.

Rita said: "Not me. I'm off tomorrow."

"I won't play Sinatra," Kay said.

"He *is* good to dance to. You can play whatever you want."

Jeff and Alvin stood and cleared the table and took the plates and glasses to the kitchen. Drew moved his chair back from the table and went toward the door, and Emily stood and walked past him and opened the door. She stepped onto the landing, and smelled the ocean in the cool air; she looked up at stars. Then she watched Drew rolling out and turning down the ramp. Kay and Rita came, and Jeff and Alvin. Emily turned out the lights and locked the door and went with Jeff down the ramp. At the van, Emily turned to face the breeze, and looked up at the stars. She heard the sound of the lift and turned to see it coming out of the van. Kay leaned down and kissed Drew's cheek, and Rita did; they kissed Alvin's cheek, and Jeff shook his hand, then held Drew's hand and said: "Monday."

"We'll be here."

Emily took Alvin's hand and kissed his cheek. Jeff pointed east and told him how to drive to the motel. Emily held Drew's hands and leaned down and pressed her cheek against his; his face needed shaving. She straightened and watched Drew move backward onto the lift, then up into the van, where he turned and went to the passenger window. Alvin, calling good night, got into the van and started it and leaned over Drew and opened his window. Drew said: "Good night, sweet people."

Standing together, they all said good night and waved, held their hands up till Alvin turned the van and drove onto the road. Then Kay looked at Emily and Jeff.

"Come for just one drink."

Emily said: "I think it's even my bedtime. But ask me another night."

"And me," Jeff said.

"I will."

"I'll follow you," Rita said.

"It's not far."

They went to their cars, and Rita drove behind Kay, out of the parking lot, then west. Emily watched the red lights moving away, and felt tender, hopeful; she felt their hearts beating as they drove.

"Quite a night," she said.

"It's beautiful."

She looked at him; he was looking at the stars. She looked west again; the red lights rose over a hill and were gone. She looked at the sky.

"It is," she said. "That's not what I meant."

"I know. Do you think if Drew was up there hanging from a parachute, he could hear us?"

"I don't know."

He looked at his watch.

"You're right," he said. "It's four o'clock."

He walked beside her to her car; she unlocked it and opened the door, then turned to face him.

"I'm off Monday," she said. "I want to go fishing."

"Good."

She got into the car and closed the door and opened the window and looked up at Jeff.

"The bluefish are in," he said. "We'll catch some Monday."

"You already have some. Let's eat them for lunch."

"Today?"

"After we sleep. I don't know where you live."

"I'll call and tell you. At one?"

"One is fine," she said, and reached through the window and squeezed his hand. Then she drove east, smelling the ocean on the wind moving her hair.

A NOTE ON THE TYPE

This book was set in a typeface called Baskerville, a modern
recutting of a type originally designed by John Baskerville
(1706–1775). Baskerville, a writing master in Birmingham,
England, began experimenting in about 1750 with type design and punch cutting. His first book, published in 1757 and
set throughout in his new types, was a Virgil in royal quarto.
It was followed by other famous editions from his press. Baskerville's types, which are distinctive and elegant in design,
were a forerunner of what we know today as the "modern"
group of typefaces.

Composed by Graphic Composition, Athens, Georgia
Designed by Brooke Zimmer